WHO SHOT *THE* SHERIFF?

II

An Original Story

By

PROLIFIC, INTERNATIONAL BESTSELLING AUTHOR

JOHN A. ANDREWS

CREATOR OF

RENEGADE COPS

THE RUDE BUAY SERIES

&

THE WHODUNIT CHRONICLES

CO-AUTHORED BY:
JONATHAN & JEFFERRI ANDREWS

Published in the U.S.A. by
Books That Will Enhance Your Life

A L I
Andrews Leadership International
www.ALI Pictures.com
www.JohnAAndrews.com

ISBN: 978-0-
Cover Design: ALI
Front Cover Deign: Mo Caicedo
Edited by: ALI
Optioned by ALI Pictures in January, 2016

THE

WHODUNIT

CHRONICLES

WHO SHOT

THE

SHERIFF?

II

The Milton Rogers' Conspiracy

TABLE OF CONTENTS

CHAPTER 1

The gray gated cell door slams shut and reverberates with a loud echo. The silhouette of two human beings linger. Burnt out fluorescent light bulbs flicker continually. Meanwhile, Bats come and go in droves, crowding the upper deck of the North Terrace cell block. Their call and echolocation peaks, while the after-sunset-rays dwindle; welcoming the beginning of dusk.

A rancid stench from this banal and dilapidated North Terrace cell-block rises amidst a gentle breeze.

Simultaneously, the simmering chatter of multiple eaves-dropping inmates perched diagonally across the way, and upstairs on both sides as well, erupts like a bee hive in distress.

Adding to all this, these insane boisterous prisoners pounce, they cheer, they chant, they chat, and they revel as if their favorite football team had just scored the winning touchdown. Not a lame dash into the end-zone but one with a zero point nine-nine seconds left in the game. In reality, there is no end-zone, no pom-pom girls, no quarter backs, no refs calling flags on the play, and of course no pig skin, just crazed inmates and cell blocks with units stacked up on top of each other. Conversely, an incarcerated newbie, not yet revealed to inmates seemed to be the main cause of prisoners going hog-nasty-wild.

Some cop multiple looksee through their tightly locked-down iron bars, while others push up against cell doors like sharks sensing some fresh human blood. Even so, revelation is still sequestered. Their bark doesn't generate a bite.

In the interim, rectangular silver and brass padlocks hanging on their gated cells, rock back and forth as a result of these inmates investigative and relentless charged-pursuit.

Yes, sizing up this newly arrived convict has become not only their priority but their utmost white-heated-obsession. In their eyes the blanketed arrival of this newbie frustrates the heck out of them. Disclosure is long overdue. Never before has inmates prowl and chant to become hitched at North Terrace. They drool like a dog desiring a bone. Their hostility and bewilderment is overbearing to say the least.

Across the way, in-front of that cell, the governing backsides of two Wardens preside. Their clothing: mid-night blue garb, decorated with green, yellow and black shoulder patches depicting Broward County Prison, is like the aroma of raw onions in the eyes of these restricted inmates, who, continually press for revelation.

CHAPTER 2

These two unorthodox Wardens, still focused on securing a big rectangular brass padlock on that cell door wouldn't let up...privacy is locked down tightly even with those flickering lightbulbs still illuminated.

For some time though the brass lock doesn't conjoin. "Snap-Click-Snap" it finally does. The lock dangles after being securely fastened. What a relief...

The two Wardens high-five each other, they buoy up, it's a *glory hallelujah moment*. They leave in high praise.

Carrying the prisoner's abandoned shackles, the shorter of two guards, FREDDIE KNOWLES is a stocky built dwarfed Caucasian less than five feet tall. His cohort is a slim fair-skinned African American woman with her backside still in obstructive view. He proceeds. She follows in tow. With his swagger he exhibits a *little Napoleonic stature*. Street chants accompany this swag-man attitude:

"Punk, it served you right!"

Knowles echoes and continues in a braggadocios humdrum. "There's no glory on the outside, but inside here can be like a living hell, Gregg Nichols."

Observing these overwrought and animated jailbirds, Knowles skillfully creates two balls with both hands using those abandoned shackles. He mimics, he steps, he elevates, he bolts, and his swag intensifies and sizzles like a new musical fusion "bap, per dap-dap, bid-de per-dap." He sticks up his right index finger high above his midget frame as an indicator he's *numero uno* and sole prison guard since Cain killed Abel. Knowles draws some applause. However, some return that index finger notion to their sender. He feels challenged.

"Chirp, chirp, chirp..." his hand-held radio interrupts the flow with clarity segued behind some intermittent-disappearing-static.

"Freddie... report to East Wing pronto ... check on inmates smoking contraband... I mean it smells like weed smoking going on the East Wing. How the heck did they get contra... up in that place? They brought in hacksaw blades in hamburger meat *inside* upstate New York, Methamphetamine in Colorado and old saw blades in Alcatraz... don't turn this into no dummy making your own "Oink" and "Oscar" show. Are they trying to brand us with some... *Bad Press*? Can't stand the bad press. Let's not repeat the Escape from Alcatraz. Not under my ... watch."

Knowles immediately collapse the chains inside one hand. It weighs...on him. He reaches for his radio now dominant on his belt with the other hand and responds:

"Copy that...Copy that Chief Myers! That new guy is uncanny like he's got voodoo written all over him. ...driving those other inmates wild...as soon as he landed in number 9."

The delayed-in-action KEISHA THOMAS has a cute face to go along with her bulged thighs. She has already secured a key ring laden with keys to her- baggy below-the-butt pants' loop. She bounces in tow trying to catch up with Knowles amidst the laughter of inmates. She hustles towards the mission.

The keys jingle, bouncing back and forth against her swift moving-in-stride bow legged and abnormal bulged thighs. Knowles propels, regains his swagger as well as her flow. He feels as though he's back in his stride again and elevated above the prison universe.

"Darn, that is some good shit!"

"Yeah!" Says his singular unit, still lagging in the distance.

Catching up with Knowles is a challenge now for Keisha. She immediately unhinges her baton, swings it high above her head like a propellant dividing the dense air saturated with clouds of smoke, while whistling loudly "I did it my... way."

As these two Wardens complete what looked like a time consuming we-got-you-sucker formality and move out of view from the cell inside the abbreviated cul-de-sac. The number 9 on the cell door becomes visible. The for some time now hidden attraction - GREGG NICHOLS' is not only revealed to his unrelenting neighbors but for the first time he comes face to face with this bunch of crazed inmates.

This mid 30s African American handsome male figure like a manikin has not only emerged center stage for them to see but finds himself morphed into their continued laughing stock.

"Turn off the lights and light up a candle! Also bring us Juice Simpson"

Yells one promiscuous inmate with no shirt on.

Inside cell number 9, Gregg, standing erect, rubs his nose continually to lock out the mixed pong emanating from his surroundings. The strong BO and chronic weed fumes saturates the air and escalates like gray scattered clouds traveling upwards to heaven in the distance.

Meanwhile, mean-spirited penetrative looks from those inmates housed in double-decker cells across the way, still taunts the heck out of Gregg to no avail. To ease the tension, he looks to his left and then to his right. Even so, he finds no relief from their oppressive twits.

Those prolonged looks, some provocative, and a few welcoming, while others are downright complicated and counter-friendly. The latter, as if to say: *inside here, in this man's world of incarceration, criminality, and flames... On this North Terrace ya block: you are our next victim, Greg-o-ry.*

In Gregg's mind he could not only see them racing through the corridor to join that weed smoking party but sawing off that rectangular padlock on his cell door with hacksaw blades and in hot pursuit.

In their eyes they see themselves taking turns - victimizing the heck out of Gregg.

His nervous thoughts rattle and submerge underneath his breath: "I can't trust none of these pricks...such scumbags, sex deprived creatures and happy-handed faggots. Can't trust the system either. Who can be trusted? They've put me in here in order to terrorize the heck out of me."

As if Gregg has been smoking marijuana too, paranoia sets in from his imaginary high... he sees himself floating in mid-air like a runaway kite across the galaxy's Milky Way.

Trying to find a level headed composure; Gregg stares at his neighbor's soiled and wrinkled prison garb. He zones in.

Gaining focus and clarity, he reflectively admires his clean and neatly pressed blue prison attire. Superiority sets in on his behalf, and he gently unbuttons his collar, sticks out his chest, and profiles for them with the confidence of a Stallion.

A few smiles are in order from his fellow convicts. Even so, Gregg Nichols does not buy into their sentimentalism. In his mind and rightfully so they are not to be trusted. He remains still non-verbal, like a brick and still not trusting: not even the air they exhale or the content inside their heart. He chooses not to become one bit unraveled- externally.

Some spew out their saliva at Gregg. Some call him a pussy, others call him a pleasure.

Suddenly, someone yells in patois:

"Me *Mumma Gattar* and *Puppa **Raymond***! *Where are you when ma need you? Blood seed!*"

CHAPTER 3

Gregg Nichols inspects his six by ten, four dark- gray-walls, sparsely furnished abode. Graffiti lingers, no doubt etched by its last great-fisted occupant. A half made up bunk bed stares back at him. Plus, BO mixed with Lysol and mildew presents an unusual funky odor combination. Before Gregg Nichols could bask in the disparity, he hears dripping sounds - *bipp bab, bipp bap*. Looking up he sees drippy liquid running down his cell wall and on top of his cotton-plaid bed linen.

While he investigates the moisture's origin, the babble on of innumerable voices blitz his cellblock's outer limits. Through all that confusion he recognizes some declarations: some more flagrant, others in a Southern twang, as well as some in unorthodox uninterrupted patois. The huge wave of opinions subsides, and then someone coughs cynically, as if bringing more wet gravel to the beach from their adulterated throat holes.

Gregg looks up agitatedly as this trickling downpour escalates and meanders into a - *drip, drip, drip, drip.* There is still a blanket of evidence regarding: the source of liquid, the chemical composites as well as the culprit. Even so, he isn't amused as the constant drip-drip and flow of experiment number one prevails.

"What did you do Mr. GQ, shoot Sheriff John Brown and his Deputy? Then you blame it on Wesley Haynes and Milton Rogers, just because you can't get up off your *bum boo cloth* grudge and *rass cloth* prejudice? You are nothing but a play-hater and *rass* bigot."

A voice in a thick Jamaican dialect vents.

One can see nothing but hate and jealousy in the eyes of this callous inmate who calls himself The SON OF JUDAH. He's a Dreadlocks attired, coarse looking six feet plus figure. The *Dread* – as he is sometimes referred to by his peers, seems to be now standing on an apple box, which makes him pull off his new height of almost seven feet six tall. His head almost kissing the roof.

Nevertheless, Gregg ignores the rhetoric and facade of hydraulics in action across the way and focuses on his own dilemma: that stream which smells like fresh adult-human-piss tapering off on his yet-to-be-slept-on multicolored plaid cotton bed covering.

"Relax GQ, you are too ... uptight." Another disparaging voice mutters and continues after a brief pause...

"Don't believe all that hype they fed you on the outside about us up in this North Terrace. We might sound rowdy right now but we uphold standards of a mellow mood. We have never seen anyone like you up in here. So what you expect?" He scans the cellblock and then continues: "We'll be easy on you. We have earned our stripes. Up in here it's all about community: What's yours is ours after your initiation."

Son of Judah slurs.

He waits for a much anticipated response from Gregg.

None emanates.

"Bigotry! Did you Gregg Nichols shoot Milton Rogers with intention of killing him? So hear me God? No, I do solemnly swear...it was an accident you honor."

Says KYLE CHANG, who's an Asian Jamaican from the upper deck above Son of Judah and perpendicular across the way from cell number nine.

Still Gregg is stone-faced, sautéed inside what has turned out to be a game of verbal roulette. He grabs his cell door, shaking it with vengeance. Across the way in cell number 10, and noticed by Gregg for the first time: is a shiny haired Gerry-curled African American Male. "They call me CAT DADDY."

He says.

Gregg lets up to hear him.

"I am a puss and I can be your daddy. I am as lame as a Goldfish but bites like a Shark!"

Cat Daddy continues in a deep Southern twang.

"Another weirdo to deal with... They couldn't house him in Alabama, the Carolinas, Mississippi, Georgia or Tennessee?"

States Gregg underneath his breath.

Suddenly, he hears movements like that of footsteps overhead. Upstairs and directly above his compartment resides a dwarfed Caucasian named RAYMOND HYBELS, wearing washed out and dirty dreadlocks and obscure to Gregg's vision. He would rather be called Ray or Hybels...never Raymond. That name evokes the demons in him and pisses him off.

Hybels yells rhythmically and in patois as what seems like the battle of words continue:

"That neophyte shot both men and then shot Milton Rogers, who paid him to shoot the Sheriff and his Deputy. That is what I call conspiracy 101... mobster style, to *rarted*. You *alloyed* bigot."

With the reek of urine now silencing the other odors and burning like ammonia inside Gregg's nasal cavity, combined with the dwarfed sized Hybels pinned inside his imagination. The *Newbie* on the cellblock, Gregg Nichols with his *cup running over,* and piss all over his cell, lashes out:

"Let the Games begin! I say Let the...Games begin! Will the real man stand up and show his stinking face...you puss... You pissed on my bed. A puss is a puss and will always be a pussy... When dis ya dog step... the puss better go into hiding. Cause, I am worse than a Rock-wilder and a pit-bull in unison. You better go into solitary confinement before me catch you *bum boo-rass cloth.* When I leap, I am coming for your jugular."

"Me throw me corn, meh nah call no fowl. Who the cap fit let them wear it. So says Bob Marley... dead and gone and will rise up again. I believe in the Duppy... but I sure *am no* co-conspirator or no *rass cloth* Glock gunman."

Says Hybels.

Jumping up and chanting in support of Hybels, the six footer Son of Judah now off the apple box but still maintaining seven feet with every jump, yells:

"Time will tell Mr. Gunman, time will tell. You no see? By the rivers of Babylon is where I and I reside. Jah Jah... *covereth* I, and nothing shall encompass about I."

Son of Judah pauses and then continues:

"No voodoo, no hex, no necromancy can touch the *I*."

"You've got a problem too, Big Man?"

Asks Gregg looking out and into the face of *Judah's son*.

Son of Judah becomes confrontational, holding on to his gated door with both hands he becomes overly animated and imitating Gregg's previous act - settling of scores.

"If you drop those words again, we are going to have some real PROBLEMS up inside North Terrace... Real Problems, big man."

Gregg ignores him.

He continues,

"Don't talk to me about problems...I and I was raised inside West Kingston ... I was born in massive problema! Ask anybody where this ya dread come from..."

"Lunch! Lunch!" yells those same two prison officers who threw Gregg inside the slammer. Keisha Thomas parades the cell block with her male underling - Knowles in tow: Once again waving her baton high above her head she gaits.

Inmates retreat as she does so.

She hoists her ring laden with keys and unlocks the cell doors sequentially.

Inmates file out hastily towards the prison's lunchroom.

CHAPTER 4

L unch is served. The long line of crooks diminishes. These Jailbirds congregate and sit to eat around immovable chairs and tables. On each plate, a ration of steamed rice, a piece of pork, broccoli, carrots and some watered down lime juice. Before the starved and downtrodden Gregg Nichols could partake after fetching his seat, he sees an inmate in the distance waving at him with the grin of a Cheshire Cat.

Gregg Nichols avoids initial eye contact. The male subject is persistent and now more animated than before with signaling and beckoning hands thrown in the air.

Gregg Nichols remembers him from the Wesley Haynes trial.

"That blabbermouth who testified against Wesley Haynes. Another puss! Darn pussy! Whey dem find yo?"

Says Gregg once more underneath his breath this time immersed with patois, while he stays put.

Gregg looks in his direction but the *puss* has disappeared. Finally, as Gregg partakes of more grub, he sees the stalker probing towards him from inside the corners of his eyes. He lands and sits down directly at Gregg's table and partakes of the ration of food.

"Gregg Nichols, how are you? I heard you made North Terrace stand on edge... upon your arrival."

Gregg pleads the fifth.

"Remember me? MARCUS DAVIS, I heard about your incident. What a travesty? Only in America. We have a black man in the White House but things are not getting better for us as black a black race. I don't understand why bad things happen to good people like us, and it isn't ISIL, Syria or some radicalized terrorist. It's our system."

Says Marcus Davis.

Gregg Nichols once again pleads the fifth.

Marcus eats some more broccoli from his meatless plate and drinks a mouthful of that watered down lemonade like it's a thirst quencher.

"Hey, I'm on the East Terrace; you should come over and hang out sometimes. Smoke a little weed, play some dominoes... We have no problems with getting in our contra... whatever you want in narcotics we have it over there. Just bring some money with you."

Before Gregg could *thaw out*. Marcus Davis continues...

"You don't trust anyone, huh? Not even Ray Hybels... I know the feeling... 'In God we trust. In man we burst.' They should engrave the latter on our almighty dollar in Jamaica. Michael Manley and Edward Seager blew that opportunity, Portia Simpson Miller also had a chance. Now it's all about what they call women's lib. Liberate what? Now it's just like it was in the seventies when women took over...dominated the workforce. These days the have's care nothing about the have nots. People like Wesley Haynes and Milton Rogers should pay up what they owe. That will bring about true liberation as far as I am concerned."

Says Marcus.

Gregg not seeing most of his logic in that statement responds:

"Sorry, wrong man; I am not into the gossip. *I see sad stories. Hear sad stories. However, I speak no evil of my fellowman.*"

"If you want to know anything just ask me. I am better than CNN, ABC, CBS, NBC, the Huffington Post and FOX combined. I and I get all the gossip up in here. I hear about every Pre-Madonna who goes whoring or push drugs while their man is inside the Pen. I heard someone pissed on your bed and it wasn't even you. Matter of fact you had not even slept in it yet."

Says Marcus.

Gregg is furious on the inside but hums a tune to "Someone pissed on my bed but it wasn't me." He turns the piece of pork over and examines it with the plastic fork. He sticks it. It bleeds.

"I am worse than a crossed bred dog; my bark is as venomous as my bite. I latch on and don't let go."

Says Gregg as he pushes the half cooked piece of meat and rest of the meal to one side. The blood swims around on the plate and merges with the fatty liquids from the same piece of meat.

"You want out of here, huh?"

Asks Marcus Davis.

Gregg Nichols nods his head.

"Like I want to puke right now. This place not only sucks, it stinks worse than a gory cesspool."

Marcus leans in.

"Your friend Wesley Haynes still owes me that money for the undelivered shipment of chronic seized on that ship in Port Antonio. Could you get him to pay up? I really need my money, bald-head."

"Don't get me involved."

Says Gregg.

"One hand washes the other. You wash mine and I'll wash yours."

Gregg is not buying into Marcus' hand washing shallowness.

"When I get out of here, I'm going to make sure the bum-boo cloth pays up. That wretch! A thief and a scamp."

"When are you getting out of here?"

Asks Gregg.

"I am hoping to get into that witness protection program or parole, whichever comes first, as soon as I am cleared. Create a new identity for myself. Move into a plush apartment suite with round the clock security and some bad, bad dogs."

Says Marcus.

"My name is Gregg Nichols, I don't have an AKA, never needed one. Don't even have an "A" in my name. I only use "K" as a short form of okay whenever I text. I just wanted to be a good husband to my wife and a great dad to our two daughters, Raina and Rayan. I don't need to be drawn into all this drama."

Marcus looks away scanning the perimeter.

"How does that thing work for an innocent man?"

"No. Only the guilty. It could have worked for Wesley Haynes, Milton Rogers and Bill Parsons, those bastards."

Says Marcus.

"What did you do to end up in here, Marcus?"

"Never let your right hand know what your left hand did. Just in case it turns into a rat. You know those boneless ones which crawls underneath doors?"

States Marcus Davis.

"You've got *it* wrong. Matthew 6:3-4 KJV: But when thou doest alms, let not thy left hand know what thy right hand doeth: That thine alms may be in secret: and thy Father which seeth in secret himself shall reward thee openly. And yes, I know a rat when I see one."

Gregg replies.

"Lunch is over!"

Yells Keisha Thomas pacing in circular motions.

"Why you say that?" Gregg says in Ebonics. "Those guys were outstanding citizens. They meant well."

Continues Gregg Nichols as both men get up from the table.

"To be continued."

Responds Marcus Davis.

CHAPTER 5

The next afternoon Deja visits Gregg at North Terrace for the very first time. Sad but elated she is seated inside the visitor's center on a wooden bench, while Gregg is brought from his cell block by Knowles. As she waits and looks around the perimeter, that pale look she exhibited since Gregg's incarceration – becomes magnified. Her mindset of coping with the entire judicial bureaucratic process, while playing the role of a single mother for their two daughters Rayan and Raina, and much more: haunts her. She envisions: *Something has got to change and soon.*

Inside this sitting room which accommodates a few inmates as well as visitors, the Nichols couple seek for privacy but finds none. Gregg's mindful: Everyone eavesdrops on each other's conversation and then lie like maggots inside nuts when they congregate.

Additionally, visible and invisible cameras capture every move made by inmates. Starved sexually, the two kiss passionately like the aftershock of a first kiss. As if by magic cameras come in tight on their upper body just in case Gregg swallows saliva and anything else with it. Bottled water? Non-existent.

Normally in this type of meeting between lovers at the North Terrace visiting room, if the inmate is suspected of swallowing anything in the act of kissing, that inmate immediately undergoes internal body scan for any consumed contraband whether his windpipe responds to swallowing of narcotics or not.

In the past visitors have been known to circulate drugs during a sensual kiss. Which they later pass out in their monitored feces.

Gregg asked about the kids. Deja in a subdued tone told him how much they missed him at home. "It's been like a decade since you've been away, Gregg. I bought Rayan her first training bra yesterday." At this point Gregg scans the room sizing up all the deviant inmates. He puts his finger on his lip; suggesting Deja keep those comments on the down low.

Finally, after a dull look on Deja's face, Gregg catches himself.

"You what? Do you check her Facebook and Instagram for those perverts?"

Gregg asks.

"You can't put the brakes on one's development... I've told her she is banned from social media until you come home."

"Sorry. That is something my Dad would have said. What did she say?"

"Something about *she can't leave her BFF's hanging.* One day this boy sent her a shirtless picture. She sent him back a post telling him how cute he was."

"Tell her to tell those FF's I am a double black belt, plus... Remind them when I bite I don't let go. How is my little princess, Raina?"

Gregg states.

Deja responds: "Raina sobs constantly wondering when you are coming home. This place is turning you mad Gregg. You look so pale. You were never so violent. Now you want to bite out everyone's jugular and spit it out."

"Deja, I would never had said that. It seems like you bring more violence in from the outside. Not helping me much. After all, I might bite it out and swallow it."

"Gregg, please stop your cannibalistic gestures."

Says Deja.

"Anyway, tell Raina soon. Her daddy will be home soon. And keep those perverts away from my girls."

Says Gregg.

"Really?"

Asks Deja.

"She won't even eat breakfast. She has gotten very skinny. The child misses your singing in and around the house. No daddy to serenade her."

Says Deja.

Their grip on each other's hands tighten.

They embrace.

"How are they treating you here babe?"

Asks Deja.

"This is no place for a real man to be...

The ration they feed us in here is what you would feed your dog with when you run out of dog food. At least I get a shower frequently. That might increase their water bill."

Says Gregg.

"I've heard this jail is full with *Happy Hands*. It must be hard on them, the only opposite sex they see are the female guards, right."

Says Deja.

"You are so right. That's what's up in this facility. They are very possessive..."

Says Gregg.

Deja tunes him out.

Gregg continues...

"I'll break their arm if they get to close to me or better yet bite it off. Last night, Hybels from the cell above me pissed on my bed."

"He was inside your room, Gregg? Can't you curb your enthusiasm?"

She asks double questioningly.

"I don't play that. He pissed inside his cell and the urine trickled down onto my bed."

Says Gregg.

"Oh. Okay. This is so overrated. This is yuki!"

Says Deja.

Gregg doesn't get it.

"I know. That's what our princess would say – yuk."

Says Gregg.

"Visiting hours are over!"

Says the eavesdropping pouncing pompous prison guard, Keisha Thomas, waving her baton with much jealousy in her eyes.

Gregg and Deja Nichols embrace and then she departs blowing a kiss at him in the wind.

"See you at the trial. They can't stop us, Gregg! They can't stop us!"

She yells.

He tries in vain to hold back his tears. But like a river flowing downstream they are unstoppable. So he curbs them with his shirt sleeves.

Keisha spins quickly in his direction after Deja is out of sight and briskly escorts Gregg back to North Terrace.

CHAPTER 6

A boisterous crowd gathers outside the Miami courthouse. Chants of "Free Gregg Nichols, he's innocent. Lock up the real gunman," reverberates. "It's nothing but a conspiracy," compliments those recites. Waving multi-colored and multi-designed placards, accompany those multiple-escalated-chants, echoed by Gregg Nichols' peeved and very disgruntled supporters.

Police with riot gear move in but cautiously.

Stoked TV reporters, legal analysts as well as Radio personnel are busily warming up their equipment. News editors stationed in mini-trucks record footage captured from the preliminary coverage.

Several protesters engage in discussions, thus igniting that tense first day of the trial. Even local Clerics converge, dressed in power-ties. Their female counterparts are adorned in pants suits.

This accusation has been well documented, plus recently attained viral status: *Gregg Nichols not only shot his associate Milton Rogers but he could have shot Sheriff John Brown along with his Deputy.*

Even so, Gregg has always maintained his innocence. Even though he had stated: he did not pull the trigger, the blanketed evidence still advocated he touched the gun that did.

On the other hand, Gregg's supporters still point their fingers at the court officers, ERROL CLARKE and QUENTIN DALEY.

With that said, the conjecture remains that: Daley who struggled with Nichols over the Glock 38, could have pulled the trigger of the gun and snuffed out Rogers, as he testified on behalf of his good friend Wesley Haynes. Also, there could have been some collaborating on the part of Clarke.

In any event, Gregg is the one charged with the shooting death, incarcerated, heading to trial and if convicted could rot inside the Pen or fried in Florida's electric chair.

Instantly, a black SUV pulls up, followed by a flashing blue lights sedan. Gregg's defense lawyer SEBASTIAN DAVIS leaps out from utility vehicle. He is followed by Gregg and two white collard officers. Armed officers step out of sedan. They probe the area while trailing behind Gregg, his lawyer and escorts.

The Radio and TV media now hot as an oven, poke microphones in the direction of Gregg Nichols and his entourage in an effort to cook up some hot news.

"Mr. Nichols, you have been charged with the death of your friend Milton Rogers. Others believe you could be responsible for the deaths of Sheriff John Brown and his deputy. Are you ready for what might turn out to be a three-dimensional-trial?"

Asks one overzealous TV reporter getting ready for the end-zone-reply from the defendant.

"No comment!"

Says Gregg.

"We have nothing to say. My client upholds his innocence."

Says Sebastian Davis eloquently. The entourage proceeds up the courtroom steps.

More reporters press; trying to boil him softer or in other words, squeeze a confession of guilt out of the defense team even before the Judge and the Jury are announced inside Judge Melendez's court room.

CHAPTER 7

Inside the courtroom, Gregg Nichols with looks of apprehension enters through the side door, hustled by the two escorts. They seat him on the front row next to his already settled attorney Mr. Sebastian Davis. Those two accompanying officers disperse through the same side door from whence they came and lounge inside the waiting area, after closing that door behind themselves.

Gregg Nichols looks to his right; stealing a glance of the prosecution's cast of characters. They loom large like Mt. Everest in his eyes.

MARK CONNOLLY, the District Attorney is standing engaged conversationally, he interrupts Gregg's stare with a penetrative return look.

Gregg probes. On the front row sits three other prosecution attorneys poised like vultures as they compare notes from their yellow pads.

Gregg scans further and recognizes new faces as well as some familiar ones, mainly from the trial in which Wesley Haynes was acquitted for shooting the Sheriff along with his Deputy.

Additionally, inside that same courtroom in which Gregg Nichols was charged for shooting Milton Rogers, weighty images emerge. They haunt him. Especially those portraying Milton Rogers falling backwards on the witness stand.

Trying hard to keep his mind in the moment, as if to make matters worse, the Jury Box presents itself with 12 hard-nosed individuals.

Inside the box: the seven men and five women are eager to decide his fate. The thought of a split rattles Nichols' mind like an overexcited snake. He amuses thoughts of them hanging themselves during deliberation.

In the courtroom friends and families are limited in attendance. There is no Wesley or Britney Haynes. However, his eyes linked with Collin Mattes, the lawyer who appeared in Wesley's defense. *What a brilliant job by Mattes,* as thoughts of the previous trial ran like cobweb through his frazzled mind.

Simultaneously, various officials file into this already packed to capacity courtroom. Nichols' eyes zone in on Quentin Daley, taking a seat. The infamous court officer with whom he struggled over the Glock 38 which claimed the life of Milton Rogers. A murder for which he has been charged and imprisoned. He reflects *Gregg Nichols shot and killed Rogers...* Those press clippings still saturate his mind and then indents. He mops cold sweat from his brow…

Many believed he did shoot the Jamaican Mogul. However, in the media there exists some lingering doubts, especially among Gregg's peers. Most artists cherished the notion that Quentin Daley shot Rogers in order to attain much needed heroic status. Some, even claimed: Daley believed strongly that Rogers was the gunman who shot the Sheriff and his Deputy Ron Charles. Some even claimed Daley wanted to be dubbed the next *Lee Harvey Oswald* a mystery killer. So he portrayed the character in order to identify.

Gregg replayed the shooting tragedy in his mind over and over like a worn-out-tape and saw himself coming out of the struggle with the gun in his hands. Only to be arrested moments later, escorted outside to the police car, forced inside, and driven away to the slammer. Later housed at the despicable North Terrace with these *lovers of men*.

Suddenly, as if by design to obliviously relieve him from his Déjà Vu, his lawyer nudges him in order to make room for his wife Deja who had just walked in. Dressed to the nines, she sat down beside Gregg and planted a big kiss upon his lips leaving her full red lip color imprints.

That act of sentimentalism drew massive attention from attendees inside the almost maxed out courtroom.

CHAPTER 8

The name REUBEN MELENDEZ stands out etched in gold, inside a wooden fixture on the Judge's bench. It peaks like a bull's horn. The Judge enters in statesmanlike fashion. In his late 50s, debonair, sporting a fresh haircut and of Latino heritage, he enters - announced. All rise, he takes his seat, so do the rest of the room except for multiple court officers in white shirts, black ties and visibly-shaped bullet proof vests underneath. They gait; not taking any chances.

Melendez, recognized among his peers for having a strong conviction reputation, glances over at the twelve jurors with a shallow smile, accompanied by a slight nod of the head.

The Jurors reciprocate both respectfully and modestly.

In the meantime, Melendez settles comfortably into his chair and leans forward with poise and forthrightness. This time he takes in Gregg Nichols as he begins to address.

"Men and women of the jury. A few months ago, inside this very same courtroom, Milton Rogers was shot while testifying in the Who Shot the Sheriff? trial. The fact remains that whoever shot Sheriff John Brown and his Deputy Ron Charles is still a mystery. Even so, as members of the jury, you are commissioned by the state of Florida to determine who pulled the trigger which claimed the life of Milton Rogers." His eyes connect with the Bailiff's interacting with the court reporter. "I guess we are ready?" The Judge continues.

He shuffles some paper, looks them over and then calls DA Mark Connolly to deliver his opening statements.

The Broward County DA with pomp and finesse approaches the lectern.

Ladies and Gentlemen of the jury … ONE man is on trial in this courtroom. I want that to be understood. Not several as claimed by the populous. Milton Rogers was shot and killed on Valentine's Day while testifying in a case having to do with the murder of two Jamaican law enforcement personnel: Sheriff John Brown and Deputy Ron Charles.

This court and the world at large believes you have been selected to find the defendant Gregg Nichols guilty of murder. The weapon, recovered from the crime scene was a Glock 38, owned by officer of the court Quentin Daley.

However, according to eyewitnesses, who we will hear from during the trial: Nichols and Daley were seen caught up in a struggle for that gun immediately after Milton Rogers was gunned down. There is much validity to this question: Why would a civilian struggle with an officer of the court over the officer's gun? Except to take the officer's life or the lives of other courtroom attendees.

If Milton Rogers was alive today the state of Florida could have been left with two less crimes on its hands to solve - one of which it inherited from another country.

Justice was obstructed by shooting Rogers inside that courtroom. The defendant, Gregg Nichols, having known Rogers for a long time along with his associates; had plausible cause to commit this horrific crime. Along with a probable motive to blanket evidence.

The state of Florida supports the death penalty. It is your responsibility to come up with a conviction: Sending Gregg Nichols to the electric chair is in order for the magnitude of the crime.

Mark Connolly returns to his seat.

Melendez doodles with pen and paper. He scans the courtroom.

Court officers assist while new arrivals mosey inside the court room are seated.

The stenographer is still typing away no doubt capturing and sub-texting.

Gregg Nichols converses with his defense team. He pats his defense lawyer Sebastian Davis on the back.

Melendez scans the courtroom once more.

CHAPTER 9

D efense lawyer Sebastian Davis puts pen to paper, and like a sponge, he soaks up Connolly's opening statement. Gregg Nichols steals a look at Davis' copious notes, neatly etched on a yellow notepad. Peripherally he can see his focused defense at work.

Davis had been note taking since before Mark Connolly began his opening arguments and remains diligent.

Davis wards off a pestering creepy-crawly.

"You okay?"

The concerned Nichols asks his attorney.

"I'm am okay as can be. Connolly is working hard to influence the jury. I've got this, plus the bug too."

Davis responds.

"What did the bug bring, good news?"

Asks Nichols.

"It says they don't have enough evidence to convict."

Replies Davis.

"Really?"

Asks Nichols.

Deja Nichols, freshening up her bright red lip gloss, interjects:

"We've got your back, Gregory!"

That name, seldom heard ever since his Adams apple evolved, tugs at Gregg's heartstring. He nods "yes."

Eventually, Attorney Sebastian Davis is called upon for his opening remarks. After addressing the judge, jury and court, Davis connects with his client Gregg Nichols as if to recalibrate before refocusing on the twelve fate-deciding-jurors. They are yellow pads and paper-mate pens ready. He adds some imaginary inches to his stature and delivers...

"Good afternoon your honor, jurors, court officials, as well as attendees. In this trial we find at its very core two defendants. Although both of these men are currently inside this courtroom, only one has been accused, charged and incarcerated. The other is free to roam and enjoy a life of sanity. He doesn't have to eat ration aided down his esophagus with watered down lime juice. At this moment he's still classified as a witness, that's all.

I still don't believe anyone has all the facts relating to the shooting death of Milton Rogers. Gregg Nichols and Quentin Daley are the only ones who do. Both of their hands handled that gun. The gun which fired the fatal shot. The bullet which snuffed out one of the most important witnesses in that trial...leaving us with this fiasco.

It is nothing new for innocent black men to be locked away in jail, while the guilty ones go free. This is an awakening reflection of our dissident judicial system.

Imagine, two men caught struggling for a gun after Rogers was gunned down. Yet, guilty fingers are still pointing at my client, an associate of Mr. Milton Rogers. My client has no motive for committing such a crime."

Gregg leans forward trying not to miss a word.

"My question is WHY?

Because the defendant is black?

Because he is talented?

Because he attended that trial in support of his friend, Wesley Haynes?

Because his prints were found on the gun from which that fatal bullet was discharged?

Others also touched the item now classified as exhibit one, as you will learn later in these proceedings.

Members of the jury you are faced with a difficult task… disseminating this story. With the fingerprints of several people recovered from the gun which snuffed out Milton Rogers and no real witness' statements recorded. What we are left with is share motive. Who really had a motive to kill Milton Rogers? That is the big question.

In this trial we are going to need some strong hard evidence. Not evidence manufactured, fabricated or imagined, evidence not bought and sold but original.

It is going to be tough for you the jury to point fingers at my client unless someone comes up with the real truth regarding this tragedy. The real truth and nothing but the truth.

It's no doubt, evidence will prove: my client Gregg Nichols did not pull the trigger which snuffed out the life of Milton Rogers.

Attorney Sebastian Davis connects visually with the entire courtroom, the jurors and then retires with poise.

He strolls to his seat next to Gregg Nichols. Deja looks at Attorney Davis and approves with a smile. One can see by the look on the defendant's face, he is happy with Davis heading up his case.

Judge Melendez calls for a 15-minute recess and returns to his chambers. Attendees mingle. The prosecution team huddles.

The defense chit-chat and powwow with Gregg and Deja Nichols.

Other courtroom attendees file out of the room.

CHAPTER 10

A midst the hustle and bustle of tight security, anxious North Terrace inmates entertain their visitors. Richard Hybels meets with a beauty named Yuki Barnes inside the visitor's lounge. Meanwhile, Gregg Nichols expecting no guests takes it easy scanning the newspaper inside cell # 9.

Yuki is African American in her thirties, and attired in a decoded gray sweat suit, Gray and white Nike sneakers and wearing a white Kangol hat – to match.

Both sit on a bench in semi-privacy. In the distance sits Cat Daddy drinking soda from a plastic cup. He eavesdrops.

Some jailbirds mingle; soaking up what's left of visiting hours. Some with no one to greet them mind their own business, while others try to read the lips of the visitors, no doubt looking for gossip.

"Are we wired?"

Asks Yuki scanning the vicinity.

Wired?

Asks Hybels.

"Tapped! Are you clean?"

Asks Yuki.

"No. Only being watched like a hawk by these electronic Peeping Toms. Every black bulb you see in the ceiling is a freaking Peeping Tom with Ray Ban sunglasses on."

Says Hybels, also casting an eye over the locale.

Yuki clues in; staring at the multiple surveillance cameras especially those designed as dome shaped tinted bulbs.

"They are very tight on us... Is this the making of a prison movie? Are they audio enabled or just faking us out?"

Asks Yuki.

"That would constitute: a breach of ones privacy."

Responds Hybels.

"Back to the business at hand. Are you in anyway a candidate for the Witness Protection Program, any affinity with the feds?"

Asks Yuki.

"No desire to. I would rather make my money...my way. Frank Sinatra said: *I did it my way.* Someone else said; *it's my way or the Highway.* They locked me up, that is the only relationship I have with their system. Everything else is my own business."

Responds Hybels.

"Cut the crap Richard; time is money. Okay... how much do you want and how soon do you need the stuff?

Asks Yuki.

"Fifty grams to start. If it moves well, which I think it will... you can profit big time. Contra does well inside here as soon as the word gets out...Chi Ching! After that you will *most def* have a repeat client. BTW, I have a few depots in South Beach... if you need some high heels to tread down Babylon Avenue, instead of those name brand sneaks."

States Hybels.

"I detest this place for more reasons than one. BTW, who pays on time for those drop-offs in South Beach, and especially Babylon Ave? ...cause I don't deal with IOU's."

States Yuki.

"I will text you coded locations. Just say this is Yuki and you are all set, nothing else. They will be expecting you."
Says Hybels.
"Leave my name out of it; just in case they tap into that busted screen Metro PC gadget. BTW, you need an upgrade on that signal because I don't play to lose... And am I your only supplier?"
States Yuki candidly.
"Not really. If you need an advance come see me..."
Before Hybels could finish his thought, Yuki surveys the perimeter once more and responds with concern:
"I need five thousand USD to begin. Will have to stock this shit, you know."
"You accept Jamaican dollars?"
Asks Hybels.
"In God we trust, no Jamaican, no Guyanese, no Chinese bills. They take up too much space. No 'in man we burst' ... USD only."
Cat Daddy walks over and makes a timely introduction.
"Hey baby I am Cat Daddy. Those lips of yours shine as the noon-day sun. And like butter against sun they are poised to...run."
Yuki studies the slick Gerry-curled up character, Hybels. She sees in him: nothing but a smooth talking pimp, and reasons "no wonder he's known as Cat Daddy.
He continues...

"That's what they call me. I'm like a cat and your daddy."

Yuki concurs.

"They call me Yuki."

She responds.

"Pretty name for a sister."

Responds Cat Daddy with glistening eyes.

Hybels hands Yuki a copy of the perspiration laden Miami Herald newspaper which he has been holding in his hand for the entire duration of their conversation.

Yuki smiles and departs in a flash.

Cat Daddy gleans two-eyes-full of her curvaceous backside with a smile, followed by an exclamation "darn! I wonder who's tapping that."

Returning to her car, Yuki runs into a man dressed in a suit. He's the replica of Cat Daddy accentuated with a pimp's attitude.

In her mind, could these two cats be identical twins...or is this Déjà vu?" Yuki races to her car avoiding the carbon copy. She gets in and takes off. About one mile up the road, Yuki pulls over and parks along the roadside. She leafs through the newspaper. Inside there is an envelope with fifty-one hundred dollar bills in U.S. Currency. She sticks all that cash deep inside her bra, tosses the sweaty Herald out the window, and drives away from the curb. She tunes into her favorite radio station and covers the upbeat song already in progress.

CHAPTER 11

Inside the courtroom the ambience is tense as the world is set to hear testimonies in the trial. Cameras and their operators are poised, ready to televise. Deja Nichols graces the witness stand. She looks more made up than ever and probably just entertained a spending spree. Every strand of her hair and clothing is in place. Her stylishness spells – impeccable.

Unprecedentedly the wife of the defendant debuts. Could this be the testimony to convict Gregg Nichols or the one to set him free? A widespread two-sided epiphany embellished by most in the media.

Inside the courtroom, Deja takes the oath.

DA Mark Connolly approaches the lectern.

"Good morning Mrs. Nichols."

he said as a mater-of-fact.

"Good morning Mr. Connolly."

Deja responds respectfully.

"Deja Nichols, you are married to the defendant Gregg Nichols. How long?"

"I am. Over 8 years."

Responds Deja.

"It is my understanding that you were sitting in this same courtroom on the evening Milton Rogers was gunned down."

"Unfortunately I was. What a horrific occurrence on Valentine's Day."

Responds Deja.

"Did you expect this to happen?"

"Objection...counsel is leading the witness!"

Yells Sebastian Davis.

A wave of grumbles rise from the cluster of Gregg Nichols' supporters in the court room.

"Silence in court! Objection is overruled."

Says Judge Melendez.

"Why were you in the courtroom on that evening Mrs. Nichols?"

"I was watching the trial."

"Was that visit your only visit during the entire trial? If so, why?"

"No. I have been in attendance more than a dozen times prior."

"All of those times with your husband, the defendant?"

"Objection!"

Says Attorney Davis.

"Objection sustained."

Says the Judge.

"Did you always accompany your husband to the hearings?"

"I did."

"Mrs. Nichols would you say your husband was an associate or a friend of the late Milton Rogers?"

The Judge is listening intently. So do the Jurors, the prosecution's clique, the defense's cluster and most of all the one with the most to lose – Gregg Nichols.

"I would say both."

Says Deja.

"Would you also say he was a celebrity chaser? A stalker or a con artist?"

"Objection!"

Shouts Davis, now on his feet.

"Counsel, no obstruction inside my courtroom. Please take your seat."

Says the Judge.

Davis lounges.

"Gregg was not that kind of person. He was none of the above. He was a business professional. Not a criminal in any way."

Replies Deja.

"Tell me about this business association between himself and the late Milton Rogers."

"My husband is a quality businessman. Always has been. His ties to Milton Rogers came through his love for music. Gregg loves what he does."

Gregg nods.

Deja continues.

"We owned a CD packaging and distribution company. Wesley Haynes became one of our clients after his business became too big for my boss Mr. Beckles, to handle.

We met Milton Rogers through our friend Wesley and Britney Haynes. My husband always has and always maintained tremendous respect for both men. He revered them... so to speak.

"Revered enough to take his life?"

Interrupts Connolly.

"He didn't."

Says Deja.

"How do you know that Mrs. Nichols?"

"Whenever they had an event we were always invited. I felt bad when I couldn't always attend some of their events."

"Did Gregg attend solo?"

"He did. When he returned home to me and the girls, he always shared his experience about the wonderful times spent together."

"What did he tell you about Milton Rogers' character?"

"Rogers was very comedic but outspoken. He didn't hold back his tongue. A class act."

"How did your husband feel about Wesley Haynes?"

"Objection! Mr. Haynes is not on trial. My client is."

Says Davis.

"Overruled!"

Says the Judge.

"Did Wesley Haynes and Milton Rogers always get along?"

Asks Connolly.

"As far as I know they were like buddies. Most of the time joking and cutting up."

"Did your husband get along with both Haynes and Rogers?"

"He did. He was like their water carrier…always willing to serve."

Says Deja.

"Did you see your husband shoot and kill Milton Rogers or did he tell you he did?"

"No. I did not see him shoot Milton Rogers and he did not tell me he did so. This is all a conspiracy to keep my husband behind bars. Our system continues to set a bad precedence for black men. One which is destroying our kids. Gregg needs to see our two daughters grow up. This system is like a leech sucking out the vim out of too many black families. This has got to stop. I want my husband home with me! Not in prison humiliated by a bunch of homos."

"Thank you Mrs. Nichols. No further questions."

Gregg smilingly and then with tears running down his cheeks gives thumbs up to Deja. The jurors reads into that emotional exchange between the couple.

Deja glances at the Jury Box and tears up.

Connolly is back at his seat.

Judge Melendez looks at his watch. Attempting to take a recess, finally…

"This case is adjourned until tomorrow at 10:00 AM."

Deja steps down from off the witness stand. She embraces her husband Gregg while shedding additional tears.

Gregg consoles her as his tears fall moistening her fancy hairdo.

Two escorts rush through the side door into the courtroom. They accompany Gregg, rushing him through that that particular courtroom exit.

CHAPTER 12

B ack at North Terrace Longue, the contended mingle, and the stressed – stress. Gregg Nichols and Marcus Davis face-off in a domino game usually designed for four players. Even so, the duo square up for what could be a friendly game. There's no money on the table and no contraband underneath.

Marcus shuffles the deck methodically. Then shoves the deck in Gregg's space, subsequently he removes the double blank from the stack as if it was marked or X-*rayed* by him. He pushes it next to Gregg's right hand.

Gregg eyes that move by Marcus disputably. Marcus draws seven cards. Gregg does the same. Marcus pushes the remainder of the cards to the other side of the table. The remaining thirteen cards nest up close to double blank.

"How did you know which card was the double blank? Did you mark the cards?"

Gregg asks.

"Funny you should ask that. These are not my dominoes, you saw me borrow them from the recreational center. Didn't you? Just play the hand you have. You have double six? Only amateurs study the game so long. It's easy Math...just aim and shoot. So play Mon."

States Marcus.

Gregg still stares at the double blank while scanning the dominoes in his hand.

"As far as you I know. If I were you I would really study what double blank means. It might come in handy. A blank is a blank. Will always be a blank. A blank from blank leaves nothing. Double six, play."

"How do you know I have Double six? Do you know something I don't?"

Says Gregg while posing double-six.

"Double six at you. Go to the pack!"

Marcus has no choice. He searches through the residual domino cards. He accumulates. Finally, he comes up with a six-ace which he slams down on the table as if it was a hot piece of coal briskly discharged from his right hand. He even blows on his hand after the card lands on the granite table top.

Gregg takes a sip from the bottled water next to him. Marcus follow suits from a larger bottle.

"Let me drink my gallon. Before Simon Peter walks on it." Marcus downs most of it, still staring at six-ace nestled up against Double six.

"You got me on that one Gregg. I hope you can be that good when you testify in court." Says Marcus.

"If I testify."

Responds Gregg.

"Deja did a great job on the witness stand. I am sure the world is waiting to hear from you."

"Yep...Deja was brilliant. She has more to go."

"You are not going to? You've got to cover your own A... She can't do it for you. You depend on a woman to save you? Understand, you are not a Wesley Haynes. If you had the money and the fame he has, you would most *def* have a chance at a non-guilty verdict without testifying...but?"

Gregg plays Double-ace.

"I'll cross that bridge when I get to it. Six ace...still your play...You pass?"

Responds Gregg.

"Me pass? Never!" Says Marcus.

"Well play *mon* ...you are holding up the game. What happen? Six ace! You cooled off? Is that why you drank the gallon of water?"

Marcus starts singing 'Like a Bridge over troubled waters' as they continue. Now he has no choice but to study the game.

"You know Milton Rogers built those restaurants with drugs money?" Asks Marcus.

"Really?'

Asks Gregg.

"You never saw his investment portfolio? The man was loaded like a freight train."

"No."

Says Gregg.

"That's why he derailed. Rogers always presented himself like a Donald Trump. Never knew his closet was full with extortion and excess baggage."

"Did you really waste him, Gregg? Tell the truth, it's just between me and you." States Marcus Davis.

Gregg Nichols is deep in thought. He stares at the double-six card which he posed and the six-ace which Marcus played later. He drops the Ace-deuce on the table and slides it up against Double ace.

"My play before yours. You must wait your turn."

Marcus goes to the deck in search of a matching domino card. He comes up with Six-deuce.

"Deuce to you. Play now." Marcus stands up, excited.

"Clap your hands if you pass."

Gregg slams down double Deuce and blows the imaginary steam off his playing hand.

"Eight bullets! Seven missing. I just wished there were more bullets inside that Glock."

Responds Gregg Nichols.

"Rogers was a big deal. They said the Feds also wanted him dead." Says Marcus.

"Why are you staring inside my hand, Rasta? You can't play a friendly game with cheating?

Asks Gregg.

"Once a man, twice a child." Says Marcus.

"Enough of your parables." Says Gregg as he throws in his hand, and merges all the cards on the table close to Marcus' hands.

"I see one man who can't stand the truth."

Gregg gets up and sticks a hand in Marcus' face.

"Lockdown!!"

Yells prison guard Keisha Thomas waving her baton high as usual and strutting her stuff. She subsequently gathers up all the dominoes. Gregg Nichols heads to the North Terrace while Marcus Davis saunters to the East.

Gregg Nichols spits his second song since incarceration: *If those walls could talk* on his way to his cell block. Inmates listen pressed up against their cell doors. Some are mesmerized, some mimic, others are muted. Subsequently, the lights go out.

CHAPTER 13

Inside Judge Melendez's courtroom, Deja Nichols continues her testament with poise and diplomacy. Defense attorney asks: "Mrs. Nichols, what is your current profession?"

"I am a singer first, entrepreneur second and mother third."

"What kind of entrepreneur are you?"

"CD packaging and distribution."

"What genre of music?"

"I sing mostly R & B, some reggae. Every now and then I'll drop some funk."

"I've heard your R & B and Reggae, never your funk."

"You've heard 'Mind your own business Mr. Babylon. It's a fusion."

"Not yet."

Says Davis.

"It is epic, its branded, my own IP... don't worry."

Says Deja.

"Tell this court about your second vocation."

Says attorney Davis.

"Gregg and I own a CD packaging and distribution company. We both have worked in that field for over five years."

"Profitable?"

"Yes. Our business exploded in the last year of operation."

Says Deja.

"You have a few major clients? I am sure."

States Davis.

"Yes."

"Wesley Haynes being one of them?"

"Objection!"

Says Connolly.

"Objection sustained."

"Yes. We took on Wesley Haynes as a client last year just before he won the Grammys."

Says Deja.

"Did Haynes bring his business to you or did you solicit his business?"

"I had introduced Wesley Haynes and his wife Britney to my ex-boss Mr. Beckles when they were trying to get their first song produced. That song turned out to be a mega hit. I guess they wanted to give back, so they approached us with their CD packaging and distribution needs."

"Are they still in your Rolodex?"

"They are."

Responds Deja.

"Milton Rogers?"

Asks Davis.

"He is still in our Rolodex. He will always be."

Says Deja.

Gregg gives multiple supportive nods.

"How did you meet Milton Rogers?"

"When Wesley and Britney Haynes' first song went platinum we were invited to the celebration which was held at his restaurant in Kingston. We had a blast. There we met Milton Rogers for the first time. He introduced himself and asked if we were enjoying ourselves. He treated us with much respect and kind hospitality. He's very businesslike but such a gentleman."

"What was your husband's relationship with the Milton Rogers after that meeting?"

"Gregg always had the utmost respect for Mr. Rogers."

"He did?"

"Yes."

"Would you consider Gregg a gunman or a water-boy?"

Deja laughs.

"Gregg couldn't shoot a fly!" She yells sarcastically.

"Does your husband own a gun?"

"Gregg does not. He's not a violent person. I don't think he knows how to pop one off. He only does karate on rare occasions. Like a sponge, one has to squeeze that craft out of him. He sure can hurt you like that with his eagle and his snake."

Says Deja.

"Did he discuss with or conspire with you in any way to end Milton Roger's life."

"No he did not."

"You were sitting next to him in that courtroom. Did you see him shoot and kill Milton Rogers? What did you see, Mrs. Nichols?"

"Gregg jumped up from his seat and wrestled with the court officer. Rogers went down. Gregg was persistent in trying to take that gun away from the court officer."

"Did he tell you why he wrestled with the court officer?"

"Gregg didn't know if he was going to shoot us next. Or on the other hand, shoot everyone else in the courtroom. Man was acting like a psycho...I've seen moves like those on TV."

Says Deja.

Judge Melendez leans forward in his chair, relaxing his torso.

"Mrs. Nichols, I have no further questions."

Says Davis before returning to his seat.

"Thank you Mrs. Nichols."

Says the Judge.

Deja retreats to her seat next to Gregg in acceptance of his husbandly approval.

CHAPTER 14

The Court Announcer calls Detective Mike Jones to the stand. He swears to tell the truth and sits down. DA Mark Connolly connects viscerally with the jury before approaching the lectern. Jones is attired in a nice black with gray pinstripes suit, a white shirt and a dapper paisley tie. He sports a new faded haircut.

The jurors buoy up.

"Good afternoon Detective Jones."

Says Connolly.

"Good afternoon."

Responds Detective Jones.

"A case of Deja Vu, I must say."

Connolly continues.

"It certainly is...twice in six months. Same courtroom, almost the same crowd except for a few new faces."

Says Jones.

"What were you doing in this courtroom on the evening when Milton Rogers was shot and killed?"

"I had been assigned along with my partner Detective Paul Stevens to the Who Shot the Sheriff? case."

"And what happened then?'

"During Milton Rogers' testimony, a gun shot went off. Milton Rogers reacted to being hit; blood flowed from his chest. He fell over backwards holding his chest. His hand was saturated with blood. My partner sitting on the row in-front me yelled:
'Unbelievable! Unbelievable! This is … Unbelievable.'
We raced to the two men still struggling over the gun at the rear of the courtroom. We discovered later the two men were Gregg Nichols and court officer Quentin Daley. Nichols had the gun pointed at Daley when we arrived. We commanded him to drop the weapon on the floor. He hesitated, then tossed it to the side."

"What type of firearm was it?"

Asks Connolly.

"A Glock 38."

"Who owned the Glock 38, detective?"

Asks Connolly.

"The gun was assigned to Quentin Daley, one of the court officers on duty during the trial."

"Do you know who fired the fatal shot from that gun which killed Rogers?"

"I am not sure. However, Nichols' body language indicated he was the aggressor in the gun struggle."

"Objection...speculative!"

Says Davis.

"Overruled."

Says Melendez.

"What happened after that?"

"Moments later we escorted the nervous Gregg Nichols to our cruiser in handcuffs. After driving him to the station we booked him."

"Nervous?"

Asks Connolly.

"Yes!"

Responds detective Jones.

"In your career you have encountered several nervous offenders like Nichols. Haven't you?"

Asks Connolly.

"Yes. Wesley Haynes was a prime example."

Wesley Haynes sitting to the rear of the courtroom shows disapproval.

"Thank you detective Jones, I have no further questions."

Says Connolly.

The Judge announces a brief court recess.

CHAPTER 15

The trial reconvenes with Defense attorney Davis pressing Detective Mike Jones. The veteran cop is very much up to the test; sitting comfortably in his seat.

Deja Nichols once again freshens up her bright red lip gloss. Her lips glitter under the courtroom light. From her purse she removes her mirror for validation of her beauty.

"Detective Jones earlier you testified: you saw
nervousness on the part of the defendant Gregg
Nichols moments before Milton Rogers was shot. Are
you an expert on body language?"
Asks Sebastian Davis.
"I would not say I'm an expert but I do understand
this reflective trait in criminals. Thus, leading to
multiple arrests and multiple convictions."
Says Jones.
"Really?"
Asks Davis.
Detective Jones hesitates.
Attorney Davis goes to his notes. He postures, he
ponders.
"Detective Jones, in the recent case Who Shot the
Sheriff? You arrested Wesley Haynes... Isn't that so?"
Asks Attorney Davis.
"I did."
"However, you claimed that you observed and I quote
'his guilty body language' which gave you reason to
believe he committed that crime."
"Yes I did."
Says Jones.
"But he did not."
"He didn't?"
Asks Jones.
"You attended the trial didn't you? Citing that
case, the defendant Wesley Haynes was found
not guilty. How come?"

Asks Davis.

"That's what they said. I still don't buy it."

Says Jones.

"So detective you have reasons to believe otherwise?"

"I do... Justice was not served in my opinion."

Says Jones.

"Opinions are like noses; everybody has one. Different size, different shape, different color."

Things seems to be getting out of hand as both are engaged sarcastically but the Judge refuses to let them ramble on.

"What grades did you receive in your Criminology-Body-Language-Class, Detective Jones?"

"Objection!"

Says Connolly.

"Objection overruled."

Says Melendez.

"Are you aware detective Jones: body language could be a facade and isn't transparent enough to be used as evidence in a court of law?"

"Objection!"

Once again the objection is overruled by Judge Melendez.

"Detective Jones, you stated earlier you were assigned to the Who Shot the Sheriff? case."

"Yes I did."

"You did, you did, or you didn't... which one?"

"I didn't."

"According to your recollection what was the result of that trial?"

"Objection!"

Yells Connolly.

"Objection overruled. Answer the question." Says the Judge.

"Wesley Haynes was found not guilty. He should have been retried"

Says Jones.

"That is a pretty fanatical statement, I must say from a law enforcement officer. Thank you detective. I have no further questions, your honor."

Says Sebastian Davis who strolls back to his seat with a swagger in his strut.

The afternoon in Judge Melendez's courtroom finished with Jones feeling the venomous sting of those brutal jabs from defense Attorney Sebastian Davis and vice versa.

DETECTIVE PAUL STEVENS WAS next to testify. He supported most of Det. Jones' testimony. Except, Attorney Davis asked him if they were hungry to attempt convicting another artist; seeing their efforts failed in the previous Wesley Haynes' trial. To which Stevens replied with a straight face: "No. We were just doing our jobs."

After a series of objections by Connolly. Attorney Sebastian Davis encapsulates his cross-examination by saying:

"I love police business when they serve and protect. However, I have a terrible distaste for bad, rancid and rotten police business."

Connolly questions Detective Stevens later in the trial, mainly to corroborate Detective Jones' sparring testimony with the defense.

CHAPTER 16

Quinten Daley was the next witness called on to testify. Grumblings from various courtroom attendees emitted before court officer Quentin Daley arrived in front of the witness stand, sends a message of justice wrongfully administered by the system. However, those clatters ceased as the evictor readies himself to intercede.

It was obvious most of the court awaited this moment. If Nichols was not going to testify, at least they were privileged to hear from the next accused...however, not charged.

"Do you solemnly swear to tell the truth, the whole truth and nothing but the truth, so hear me God." the bailiff eloquently articulated.

"I do."

Says Daley.

Once again anti-murmuring erupts from the defense's section of the courtroom.

DA Mark Connolly approaches and begins cross-examining of Quentin Daley, the prized eyewitness.

"Mr. Daley, you were the court officer on duty when Milton Rogers was murdered inside this courtroom on Valentine's Day of this year, wasn't you?"

"I was."

Mr. Daley your passport was stamped by Jamaican immigration indicating you visited that country between August 1st and 16th last year. The Bailiff brings the passport over to Daley. "Is this your passport?"

Asks Connolly.

Daley examines it.

"Yes, this is my passport.

"Were you in anyway involved in the previous incident: the shooting death of Sheriff John Brown and his Deputy Ron Charles on August 12th?"

"I was not. It wasn't me."

"Do you know anyone who might have been involved?"

"Objection!"

Says Sebastian Davis.

"Objection sustained."

Says Melendez.

"No. I do not."

Says Daley.

"What was the purpose of your visit to Jamaica in August of last year?"

"I was on vacation with my wife and our teenage son. Jamaica had been on our vacation wish list since we honeymooned there over a decade ago."

Responds Daley.

"You had a great time?"

"Yes we did."

"Did you collaborate with Milton Rogers on this trip regarding any criminal activity? and as far as you know was he involved in that double shooting of the Sheriff and his Deputy?"

"I don't know if he was. I had never met Mr. Rogers… Never heard of him until the trial."

Says Daley.

"Do you know if Gregg Nichols was involved in the shooting of the Sheriff and his Deputy?"

"I do not know if he was. He resided in Jamaica at the time burning CDs and other business… who knows what else."

"Did you know Gregg Nichols before Milton Rogers was shot and killed. Did you hung out with him, smoked a joint or two maybe? Drank a beer, played dominoes. Any involvement you can recall?"

"No. I did not know Gregg Nichols prior to that shooting. Like I've stated: That was the first time I met Gregg Nichols when he removed my gun from its holster by surprise and shot Milton Rogers."

"So when he grabbed your gun from you, that was the first time you met the defendant?"

"Objection."

Says attorney Davis.

"Objection overruled."

Says the Judge.

"Did you give the gun to Gregg Nichols to shoot Rogers or did he grab it from you, officer Daley?"

"He took it from me... grabbed it!"

"Liar...I tried to stop you from shooting him."

Says Nichols rising up out of his seat and pointing in Daley's direction.

"Order in court." says Melendez.

Nichols returns to his seat.

"How many rounds did he discharge?"

"One round."

"How come?"

"That's all I saw."

"Mr. Daley, was your gun fully loaded before Milton Rogers was shot with that same gun?"

"No it was not. Partially..."

"How many bullets did you recall loading inside that gun?"

"Seven."

"And you say seven out of eight inside that magazine was partial?"

"Yes!"

"Was that partially loaded gun a planned activity or some of those bullets just happened to be missing at that time? Did they fall out of the gun when you opened it and you forgot to put them back inside?"

"I am not aware of any bullets falling out of that gun."

"And Mr. Daley... you didn't plan it that way to be accosted by the defendant ? Did you?"

"I did not."

"Did you shoot Milton Rogers?"

"No. I did not."

"Well if you didn't Mr. Daley, Who did? Who positioned themselves and pulled the trigger?"

"The defendant Gregg Nichols. He shot Rogers."

"Whose gun did Gregg Nichols use to commit that brutal murder?"

"Mine."

"How? I mean how did he do it?"

"He grabbed my gun away from me, opened the magazine, inserted his own bullet and shot Milton Rogers."

"So he used his own bullet, he didn't trust yours to do the job... taking out Rogers?"

Gregg is agitated.

"Liar! Liar! That is highly impossible."

Says Gregg Nichols.

"Silence in court."

Says the Judge striking his gavel.

The murmuring residue fades to the emittance of a pin-drop sound which emerges swiftly and resides.

Heads turn to see what caused the dead silence.

"Counselor, you may continue."

Says Melendez.

"So your gun could have been tampered with prior, and apparently left empty?"

"Possibly."

"By whom?"

"I have no idea."

Responds Daley.

"Did you share information regarding the status of your gun with the defendant or anyone else?"

"No. I had no communication with anyone regarding my gun."

Says Daley.

"Mr. Daley, did the defendant push or shove you in an effort to wrestle your gun away from you?"

"No. He did not. He grabbed me by the seat of the pants. Lifted me up off the ground and took my gun away."

"What did you say to him?"

Asks Connolly.

"You need to back off and return to your seat. Don't try anything funny or you'll be dead meat."

"Did you reach for the handcuffs which you carried, as an officer of the court?"

"No. There was not time enough to do so."

Connolly signals the court bailiff to the square next to the Stenographer. On the table bailiff retrieves a large envelope. Connolly opens the package. Bailiff takes out a Glock 38, un-holsters, and checks it to make sure it isn't loaded. It's not. Safety is administered. Bailiff hands it to Connolly holstered.

Connolly un-holsters.

"This is a Glock 38, the same ammo recovered at the scene after the fatal shooting. Does this look like the gun you carried, and was taken away from you when Milton Rogers was shot inside that courtroom?"

Says Connolly.

"Objection. May I approach your honor?"

Says Davis.

"Yes. You may." says the Judge."

Sebastian Davis approaches, removes his smart phone and takes multiple pictures. So do other lawyers representing both the prosecution as well as the defense.

All picture takers return to their seats.

"Counsel may we proceed with your cross-examination?"

Asks the Judge.

Connolly hands the gun to Quentin Daley.

"Looks familiar? Are you sure this is the gun?"

Asks Connolly.

"It does."

Responds Daley.

"Please show this court and the jurors where your gun was when it was taken away from you by Gregg Nichols." Instructs Connolly as he now passes the gun's holster to Quentin Daley.

Daley puts on the holster and positions the gun inside of it. Gun and holster are attached on the right side of his pants' waist.

"This is where my gun was positioned, when the defendant snatched it away from me."

Says Daley pointing confidently to the right portion of his waist.

"Did the defendant point it toward you before he shot Milton Rogers?"

Asks Connolly.

"No. He grabbed the gun away from me, loaded it and immediately shot Milton Rogers after loading."

"No further questions."

Says Connolly and strolls back to his seat.

"Mr. Davis, your witness."

Says Judge Melendez.

CHAPTER **17**

S ebastian Davis approaches. Firstly, he studies the Quentin Daley like a text book. Secondly, he connects visually with the jurors and rest of the courtroom. He cross-examines…

"Mr. Daley, what was the purpose of your trip to Jamaica in August last year?"

"As I have already mentioned, I was on vacation with my family."

"Which hotel did you use for that trip?"

Asks Davis.

"Sandals."

Replies Daley.

"Sandals? Must have been one heck of expensive vacation."

"It was!"

Responds Daley.

"Who picked up the tab, your contractor? Very coincidental; so you showed up in Jamaica right about the time Sheriff Brown and his Deputy were shot and slain. A vacation you stated earlier you postponed for at least five years. Months after you returned a prominent Jamaican was gunned down inside a court room under your watch. Do you expect us to believe you had nothing to do with these crimes?"

States Davis.

"I have already taken an oath. Didn't I?"

Responds Daley.

"Mr. Daley, how many bullets were inside the chamber of your gun when Milton Rogers was shot?"

"That is a hypothetical question. Are you asking me about before he was shot?"

"Did you fully load your gun before attending the trial that day?"

Asks Davis.

"I did not."

"Why not, Mr. Daley? You were an officer of the court, and functioning in a high profile case. Why would you choose not to fully load your gun to protect the courtroom if necessary?"

"When I picked up the gun I thought it was loaded as I left it the day before."

"You assumed? Do you not brush your teeth in the morning, instead of claiming it was already brushed the night before?"

"My gun has always remained in whatever condition I left it."

"Mr. Daley, you mean to tell me, as an officer of the court, you show up at a trial, not knowing if your gun was loaded. Secondly, if there were multiple rounds inside your gun chamber. What if you had to discharge multiple rounds to protect the entire courtroom? This is America... what if you had to deal with a lone wolf? Or did you deliberately put one bullet inside the gun so you can shoot Milton Rogers and as you were confronted... *click click* – empty gun. So you saved yourself from getting shot? Just like in the movies, huh?"

"I don't know what you are talking about. My gun is normally fully loaded."

Says Daley.

"But it wasn't on this occasion. You stated earlier it was partially..."

"It was. I believe..."

Responds Daley.

"You believed but it was not a fact. Do you believe you have your car keys on you or do you know that for a fact?"

"I know that for a fact."

Responds Daley.

"Mr. Daley, you earlier testified: *my gun is normally fully loaded.* Those are your words. However, it wasn't. Plus you either failed to check it or it was already your knowledge: that the gun was fixed with one bullet inside its chamber or you deliberately put one bullet in the gun, with Milton Rogers' name on it? You wanted to kill him execution style. Didn't you, Mr. Daley? So you planned it, executed, and boom!"

"Objection."

"Objection overruled."

Says Melendez.

"How many bullets were inside your gun chamber before Milton Rogers was shot?"

"I don't know. Don't recall. I know that Gregg Nichols tampered with its chamber prior to shooting Rogers."

"According to the ballistics report, your gun was empty after discharging the bullet which claimed the life of Mr. Rogers. That would imply mathematically it contained one bullet prior to discharge. Evidently, you could not miss. You must have shot many bulls-eye at the shooting range. Yes?"

"I don't know how many shots were fired at Mr. Rogers because I did not shoot him."

"Who did Quentin Daley? Who did? Tell the court they are waiting for your answer."

"Gregg Nichols did."

"Did he eat the rest of the bullets which he found inside your gun chamber?"

"I don't know that?"

Says Daley.

"Whose responsibility was it to make certain the gun you were carrying during the trial was fully loaded?"

"It was mine."

"What you are telling the court is basically it was negligence on your part. You expect us to buy into that? Like your unscheduled trip to Jamaica back in August."

"I have told you the truth."

Says Daley.

"Thank you Mr. Daley. No further questions."

Judge Melendez strikes the gavel.

"This trial will reconvene tomorrow at 10:00 AM!"

CHAPTER 18

L egal Analysts and other news media descend on courthouse grounds like starved flies onto molasses. They buzz over each other in order to report the news. Attendees exiting from the full to capacity courtroom are mesmerized by such historic media commotion. The growing noise of confusion covers the entire courthouse sidewalk.

Finally, a legal analyst burrows through the crowd and foray on Quentin Daley who is encircled by an entourage of lawyers.

"Mr. Daley, you finally got your chance to testify in court, in an uncanny case which many have dubbed - a Milton Rogers' conspiracy. How do you feel now that you've shared your side of the story?"

"I feel great. Finally got the monkey off my back."

"Sure must feel good."

Says the reporter taking back the microphone.

"If you had to do it all over, you would be sure to check your gun to ensure it was fully loaded. Wouldn't you?"

Reporter hands microphone back for Quentin Daley's POV.

Multiple microphones are now perched in Daley's face to receive the answer to this all important, loaded question.

"I would. You know things happen. If it was fully loaded, I might not have been here today. On the other hand, Nichols might have shot and killed me too. By far that was his intention an imminent clean sweep...the outcome could have been worse; many more lives taken."

Another analyst interrupts…

"Why didn't you say that to the judge? You claimed you were innocent. What were you afraid of Mr.

Daley? Do you still see fingers pointing at you?" The microphone is shoved back at Daley.

The other analyst regains his stride and interrupts.

"Were you hurt as Nichols grabbed you by the seat of your pants during that ordeal?"

Asks that Analyst.

"Daley, you are a wicked man. You lied on the witness stand. You shot Rogers and pinned it on Gregg Nichols. Just like you shot the Sheriff and his deputy, then they tried to pin it on Wesley Haynes!"

Yells a Nichols' non-microphone bearing supporter and legal scholar.

"That's enough guys. We've got to go."

Says one of his Daley's attorneys as he directs that multiple legal entourage off the side walk.

The lawyers rush Quentin Daley inside the waiting car.

The car departs speedily. They follow in tow.

CHAPTER 19

Gregg Nichols returns to "North Terrace" wishing the trial was ended and all those guilty fingers were pointing at Quentin Daley instead.

After entering his cell block, Son of Judah emerged like a snail out of its shell.

"Long time! You are back Gregory Nichols. When do we party...I mean really get it on?"

Gregg Nichols pleads the fifth.

Son of Judah feels ignored.

"They said you did shoot Rogers. So you deliberately shot Milton Rogers? If there were more bullets inside that gun you would have shot the court officer too. Make it a bang, bang instead of a bang. That bauy Quentin Daley: Blow *him rass cloth head off*. Wouldn't you?"

Gregg Nichols is still mute.

Hybels, invisible to Nichols. However, resides above his cell but only visible to Son of Judah and other inmates from their vantage point, says in patois: "There is a *rass cloth* trend. A sequence... You hypothetically shot the Sheriff and his Deputy, then you shot Milton Rogers. One man standing was Quentin Daley next to the gunman. If bullets were still inside the gun, that court officer would be dead too. As Judah just explained. We have to start calling you the *rass* Glockman instead of the gunman. That name fits your MO."

"He's got to have a deputy. Maybe Errol Clarke is in on it too."

Son of Judah replies.

"You are right. I've got to have two victims at once. Two caskets instead of one. Any two will do. Who will be next? I wonder who my next deuce would be...come on *deucee*, deuce. The eagle for one and the snake for the other. Who wanna test me, old schools? Piss against the wall punks." Says Nichols as he practices his karate moves, mirroring himself on the dark gray cell wall.

"Dinner!" Yells the two prison officers, changing the tense mood and the entire cell block vacates.

NICHOLS MULLS OVER HIS FOOD as he sits solo at the 4 seat round table inside the prison cafeteria. Son of Judah, Hybels and Kyle Chang walks in with their servings of ration and plops down at his table. There is dead silence.

Gregg Nichols takes a bite of the cold broccoli from his plate. He once again pushes the meat aside as if the cooks didn't get the memo.

"Calm down Nichols, we've got your back. What ever happened to your domino playing mentor, the *buay* Marcus?"

Asks Hybels.

"I heard he went to "East Wing," fixing to join the witness protection program and get to hell out of here. Is he taking you with him?"

Asks Son of Judah.

"My mother used to say: What your right hand knows never make your left hand know."

Says Kyle Chang.

"That's pearls of wisdom. *It is said never cast your pearls before swines for they will turn around and rend you.* The key word is rending. Now, he is fixing to tell on your *rass*... Don't you understand Mr. Artiste? You are confiding in a snitch. We thought you know better. Seems you didn't learn much in that department from the blind old man, Mr. Beckles.

Says Son of Judah.

Gregg Nichols reflects.

It seems like they have placed Gregg Nichols into a tight vice and tightening it gradually with their fists full of physiological witticism. Gregg examines the plastic fork methodically. The cutlery breaks during its probing investigation.

"Gentlemen, it should have been very apparent that I needed my solitude. However, seeing you joined me uninvited, and I welcomed you into my space. That says I Gregg Nichols deserve some respect. With that said, I'll prefer that you keep your comments to yourself."

All three of his neighboring inmates immediately stand up initiating physical confrontation – daring Gregg to retaliate. Gregg is about to get even.

In the interim, Keisha Thomas and Freddie Knowles moves speedily in their direction. Keisha waving her baton high, says:

"Gentlemen don't start no fire up in here. Put out that spark or all four of you are going to the hole. We are the only voice up in here. You listen to us or pay the consequence for real."

The quartet disperses back to North Terrace most swearing and in patois under their breaths.

CHAPTER 20

O utside the South Beach Bar and Grill, high end automobiles double park in lieu for attention by Valet parking attendees.
Inside the crowded facility patrons get their groove on while the DJ drops some of the latest tracks. Overlooking the bar, the large gold framed clock displays 9:55 PM. Frequenters mindful that the main attraction for the night will take the stage in five, rush

to the bar to fill up or get refills. Those seated at tables signal waiters and waitresses to serve their tables quickly.

The high fashioned Emcee takes the stage.

"Ladies and gentlemen let's give a warm South Beach, Miami welcome to the undiscovered artist but not for long - Yuki Ba-r-nes!"

Loud hand clapping and cheers follow in applause.

Yuki Barnes takes the stage dressed to the nines. She drops one number. A loud applause follows.

While the four-piece band extends the beat Yuki steps closer to the edge of the stage.

"Good evening Miami... How are you all doing South Beach? You all looking great tonight. Are you ready to party? Ha, hah hah... Man in the red shirt, looking very patriotic. I can tell you are ready. Before I lay the next couple of tracks on you, I just want to give a *big up* to Gregg Nichols over there in the Pen. Also to his lovely wife Deja, who is probably going through some tough times since he's been locked up?"

Most of the crowd raise a glass in support of Deja.

"It must be tough on that woman making a living now with her man inside the pen. No daddy for her kids. No money... No money no honey especially when you are locked away with such bastards."

Yuki tears up and gains the sympathy of women and men patrons alike. One woman rushes a box of paper tissue on stage for the artist. Yuki thanks and wipe the tears away.

"She has been a great inspiration to many. Women are made of extra stuff, aren't we?"

The audience waiting for the next song to drop applauds heartily, mostly women this time. Although a few men chime in hesitantly.

"These are some of my favorite Boss woman Deja's tracks. Are you ready? Turn it up Mr. DJ! You ready South Beach?"

Says Yuki.

Yuki Barnes sings three covers Deja style. The crowd wants more. The eager DJ pulls up the last cover dropped, as Yuki exits stage right.

Outside South Beach Bar and Grill Yuki readies to board the taxi. Fans rush towards the taxi cab. Pushing pen and paper at her. She autographs a few.

"You were great tonight. You did an awesome job with Deja's songs."

Says one skimpy dressed woman after collecting the Yuki's inscription on a napkin.

Yuki blows a kiss in the wind as customarily.

The cab takes off.

CHAPTER 21

The media has now been inundated for more than a week with news regarding the infamous witness Marcus Davis. Rumor has it: Davis recently joined the witness protection program in order to turn in mega Drug Lords from Jamaica, Colombia and Mexico who trafficked in the U.S. While some refer to him as the Snitch who tried to bring down artist Wesley Haynes during an unconventional testimony in the Who Shot the

Sheriff? trial. Still some believed Marcus Davis, known by his peers as "The Parrot" was a paid witness in that case.

Regarding the witness protection program: some advocated it was nothing but a hoax or publicity stunt concocted by Davis in order to strike a deal with his parole officer. It was believed a man who liked that much publicity, would do anything in order to get his name out there. Thus, drawing sympathy to his cause is a no-brainer.

On the other hand, in order to thwart the press, Marcus Davis claimed Wesley Haynes owed him money on a shipment of weed bound for his drug depot in Miami but never arrived. The ship "On Time" which never arrived and identified to have been carrying his shipment was seized in Port Antonio, by Jamaican police.

After that investigation of the ship's origin headed up by top cop Sheriff John Brown and Port Antonio's top brass DEA Lieutenant Graves. Wesley Haynes' whose name surfaced as co-owner of that ship, was sent to prison for ten. Haynes was later released early, after five years on good behavior.

Marcus Davis still maintained a venomous grudge for Wesley, not only because as he claimed money was owed him from the aborted shipment of weed but because of Wesley's stellar success as an international reggae artist.

With many bystanders yet to be called in this trial, it was uncertain if Marcus Davis was among them or the BFF of Deja Nichols, Britney Haynes – the wife of Wesley.

Some even claimed: Wesley Haynes would be among those witnesses. However, many still suspected his involvement. Haynes was already found not guilty for shooting the Sheriff and his Deputy. So in some minds that hatchet should be buried. Yet there were those who just couldn't let go of it. Even top intellects inside the legal arena.

Legal Analyst Bradshaw a Haynes advocate echoed:

"Even though the victim Milton Rogers was a friend and mentor of Haynes, staying out of that environment would do Haynes much justice.

Additionally, it was evident Haynes did not pull the trigger which snuffed out Sheriff John Brown and his Deputy; as he was acquitted of those charges on Valentine's day."

Yet, many non-Haynes supporters debated: his return to that courthouse and placed on the witness stand. Legally, it's not practical to try a person twice for the same crime.

"If Haynes testified on Nichols' behalf and made a single blunder or told a white lie it could be like the opening of an old wound. It was evident the masses wouldn't be tolerant with all that inflammation from a wound which should have already been healed. Rather any new cut would suffice. At least anyone who owned a similar Glock 38 and detonated a single round.

So those anxious debaters tucked their tails between their legs, at least for the time being. In other words, they cooled it.

In the meantime, one radio station broke the news that Wesley and Britney Haynes were on their way to Paris to drop their new song.

CHAPTER 22

I t is another day inside Judge Melendez's courtroom. The atmosphere grows tense as excessive movements recedes to almost zero.

The court requests Marcus Davis. He steps up to the witness stand and takes the oath. DA Mark Connolly steps into position and begins his cross-examination of Davis.

"Marcus Davis, good morning."

"Good Morning."

The witness responds.

"Second time around?"

"It is."

Marcus Davis responds.

"Are you getting paid to testify in this case?"

"No. I am not getting paid one red cent. Only here for justice to be served."

Responds Marcus Davis.

"Marcus Davis, is this courtroom familiar to you?"

"Objection!"

Says his namesake Sebastian Davis for the defense.

"Objection sustained. Answer the question."

Says Judge Melendez.

"It is. I was here on Valentine's Day."

Says Marcus Davis.

"What happened on Valentine's Day?"

"Objection. Leading the witness. Your honor we are privy to what took place."

Says Sebastian Davis who is now standing.

"Objection overruled."

The defense lawyer retreats.

"We all know what happened on Valentine's Day. How much did you know Milton Rogers?"

Asks Connolly.

"Counselor?"

The Judge cautions.

"How much? A little? A whole lot?"

Asks Connolly.

"Milton Rogers came from Mandeville. He grew up across the park from where Wesley Haynes lived. He was a smooth talker. Drove expensive automobiles. Rogers later moved with his drug pushing attitude to Kingston because of multiple threats made on his life.
"Unsubstantiated!"
Yells Nichols.
"Mr. Nichols! You may continue Mr. Davis."
Says Melendez.
"When he arrived in the big city, he immediately bought two restaurants and additional fancy rides, with hydraulic suspensions and rag tops. He upgraded and expanded these eateries just before Wesley Haynes moved to Kingston. People in Manchester and Port Antonio were after Rogers like a hawk after young chickens. They said he owed them money. However, no one in Kingston allowed anyone to turn him in, not even the cops. They revered him. When Haynes told me he was purchasing a ship with Rogers to transport weed, I laughed but wasn't surprised; I knew there would be repercussions. I saw them as two buck rats in one nest with short tails.
However, I told Haynes be careful he turned out like Rogers and spread all over Jamaica like stage-four-cancer.
Haynes went back and told Rogers what I said, that dirty dog. Milton Rogers later called and told me: I would starve. They will dry up my turf and watched

Me as I morph into a leftover pretzel, gnawed at by rodents."

"The man is lying! That snake."

Says Gregg Nichols taking a page from Wesley Haynes' book.

"On a subsequent shipment, Haynes told me to pay before delivery. I did but never received the shipment."

Marcus Davis continues.

"What happened?"

"The ship was seized in Port Antonio."

"What did you do when you found out the ship was seized?"

"I asked Haynes what's up. He gave me a *sorry* story. So I called Rogers and told him I knew he co-owned the ship and told him I need my goods or my money back. He said there is no money back guarantee in the files. The loss is a part of business and that I am not the only one suffering. When I asked him to name other sufferers. He said its confidential but Babylon is suffering too. And those who bring you news will also *sosoo pan you*."

"The ship seizure? When did all this happen?"

Asks Connolly.

"Five to six years before Sheriff John Brown and Ron Charles got shot."

Responds Marcus Davis.

"How much do you know the defendant, Gregg Nichols?"

"I know him well. We play dominoes at North Terrace. He's amateurish; waste too much time reading the game. Nichols joined the Rogers and Haynes posse right after Haynes moved to Kingston. Also frequented night clubs in Mandeville during the first half of August last year. When both Sheriffs got shot.

I recently spoke with him a few times in the Pen... He looked very discombobulated. Showed signs like he had lost his marbles."

"Marcus Davis, do you know who shot Milton Rogers on Valentine's Day?"

"No."

"Did you shoot Milton Rogers?"

"I did not."

"Did Gregg Nichols tell you he shot Rogers or conspired to do so?"

Asks Connolly.

"Objection! This is not a circus. This is a trial!"

Yells Sebastian Davis.

"Objection sustained."

Says Melendez.

"You may answer the question."

Says Connolly.

"He didn't tell me outright. However, I wouldn't put it past him. He did tell me how he wished there were more bullets inside that gun. And all he was thinking about was clean sweep, a courtroom clean sweep.

"Objection, speculation, hearsay!"

Yells Davis for the defense.

"Objection overruled. Counselor you'll have your chance."

Says Melendez.

"Did Nichols confide in you in prison."

Asks Connolly.

"He did. I thought: maybe he also had some weed on that ship which never left Port Antonio... he never said but *Birds of a feather do flock together.*"

"Your honor, I have no further questions."

"Attorney Davis, your witness."

Says the Judge Melendez glimpsing at the clock on the courtroom wall and the Jury box.

CHAPTER 23

Sebastian Davis began drilling by asking Marcus Davis if he felt he could be trusted by anyone. "Ouch!" says Marcus Davis in his mind, "no one has ever asked me that before." Marcus Davis replied after giving some thought: that many people trust him as far as he knew.

One could tell that answer didn't sit well with Gregg and Deja; by the frown on their faces.

"Really?"

Asks Sebastian Davis.

"The ones who don't trust me cannot trust themselves either." Marcus Davis continued in a rather sarcastic overtone.

The defense lawyer then asked him if he had aspirations all along to join the witness protection program. With a broad smile on his face he told the court:

"When you do good, great things get thrust upon you. However, all that program analysis stuff is still purely speculative."

Sebastian Davis then asked Marcus Davis how long since he cherished those desires to join the program. To this question Connolly objected. Nevertheless, the Judge insisted that Marcus Davis provided an answer. To which Marcus replied *"over ten years, sir."*

Sebastian Davis continued pressing his namesake about his statements made prior in testimony regarding Milton Rogers.

"Did you have a vendetta against Rogers?"

Asked the defense lawyer.

"I did not. However, I've always seen him as a small fry. Although he functioned like he was some big potato."

Says the witness.

"Watch your words!"

Says Nichols under his breath but loud enough to draw a response from Judge Melendez.

"Silence in court!"

Barks the Judge.

"The man's a liar! A blatant liar, a conspirator."

Continues Gregg Nichols.

"Gentlemen I am warning you."

Says the Judge.

One could now hear a pin drop inside the court room after that warning…with the stenographer now on hiatus and court officers ambled back into position, the Judge says:

"Please continue Counselor."

"You seemed to be at odds with Wesley Haynes, the man who you referred to as Rogers' partner. It is hard for me to believe you didn't have it up for Milton Rogers and wanted to see him get rubbed out."

"Wesley ran his mouth too much and so did Rogers, Parsons and his Water-boy Gregg Nichols."

"Were you involved in a conspiracy to kill Milton Rogers?

"No I was not. No reason to."

Says Marcus Davis.

"Do you know of anyone who was?"

"No. Rogers and Wesley Haynes shot the Sheriff. That's what's still on the street nowadays. Most-likely, someone was now after Rogers. *That's how the mop flops.*"

"What grounds do you have for that statement?"

Asks Sebastian Davis.

"Come on, it was common knowledge. Whatever you do to others will be done unto you... that's Biblically correct? Rogers was a *jennile*. He owned an Infiniti SUV and a Glock 38 just like Wesley Haynes did. Maybe the same dealer reassembled both guns? They found his Infiniti. Where is his Glock? Ok! It shouldn't take a rocket scientist to figure that one out. Two infinities could have been included instead of one. You guys are the lawyers, not me. Go figure...I don't get paid to do that stuff."

"Mr Davis were you not on parole at the time when Sheriff John Brown and his Deputy Ron Charles were gunned down? Did you visit Jamaica back in August of last year?"

"Jamaica?"

Asks Marcus Davis.

"Yes Jamaica. A stamp in your passport indicates you did."

Says Sebastian Davis.

"I was. That is my birthplace. I go whenever I choose *mon*. I wasn't born *inna foreign...scene?*"

Says Marcus Davis.

"Who did you rub out on your trip?"

Asks Davis for the defense.

"No one."

"No further questions."

Says Sebastian Davis and briskly ambles to his seat.

Gregg Nichols gives his lawyer thumbs up in approval. Deja shares smiles with both men seated to her left.

The Judge takes a 15 minutes recess which later evolves into an adjournment of the trial's proceedings for the day.

CHAPTER 24

I n Paris, after being interviewed and dropping a sample of their new hit song *Someone has got to Pay* at a studio session, Britney and Wesley returned to their hotel.

Upon entering they find themselves immersed in the Late Breaking News flashing across their TV screen: ***Woman shot in Drive-by is identified as artist Deja Nichols.***

The news broke early this morning: Last night Deja Nichols, the wife of Gregg Nichols was rushed to Mercy Miami Hospital. It is reported the artist/ entrepreneur was gunned down walking towards her car in South Beach. According to the reports: At 10:30 PM on last evening. Deja Nichols was traveling to her car and carrying an empty duffel bag.

Several bullets rang out. According to one eyewitness' account. The artist fell over backwards onto the sidewalk a few feet away from her parked BMW. A speeding black automobile departed from the scene.

That lone eyewitness an elderly man riding his bicycle after dark in the park states: he spotted a grayish black or what looked like a black car speeding away from the scene. The car displayed temporary license tags.

Deja apparently took a bullet to her right arm and was minutes later rushed to ER, where she appears to be in stable condition. Meanwhile, the drive-by assailant(s) is still on the loose. It was just a few days ago since Deja testified on her husband Gregg Nichols' behalf inside a Miami courtroom. He has been charged in the shooting death of Jamaican Mogul, Milton Rogers.

According to sources, singer Britney Haynes was distraught upon hearing about Deja Nichols' incident. The two female artists were very instrumental in Wesley Haynes' rise to fame and fortune.

MEANWHILE IN MIAMI news of the shooting incident saturates the printed media as well as Radio and TV. The Miami Herald front page headline reads: ***Woman shot in Drive-by is identified as Deja Nichols.***

Many in the media theorize, why was Deja in that area of South Beach after midnight. An area dominated by pimps, prostitutes and Drug Lords. The artist recently testified in her husband's trial.

In the meantime, her very close friends Wesley and Britney according to sources inside the Haynes' camp, are on the way back from an abbreviated trip to Paris. Where they just signed a mega deal for their next album: *Someone has got to Pay.*

Britney Haynes is a potential witness for the defense in the case surrounding Milton Rogers' death.

Deja was very instrumental in helping Wesley and Britney Haynes in landing the contract for their first song which became a mega hit.

Gregg Nichols picks the news up at breakfast inside the North Terrace lunchroom, headlined in the Miami Herald. He is pissed and almost drowning in tears. Several make-believe supporters huddle around him including, Hybels, Chang and Son of Judah. Instead of talking to Gregg they converse with each other in an unknown tongue, gesturing and using sarcasm.

The news repeated itself across many major Radio and TV networks: "Meanwhile, Miami police are looking for the vehicle in question along with its suspect(s) who are still at large. If you have any information regarding the shooting incident you are asked to contact Crime Stoppers immediately."

CHAPTER 25

L ate breaking news concerning the shooting of Deja Nichols continue to predominate the media. Upon hearing the summary from other inmates, Gregg Nichols becomes more rattled and unnerved. He mentally aches from its venom and immediately goes into solitude. He envisions: not only there's no Deja by his side inside the courtroom but his two daughters ages seven and nine having to be without the company of their mom and their dad for a while. He is granted permission to one telephone call per day. Even so, when he calls home, no one picks up. "Whatever could go wrong just did," he mutters underneath his breath after hanging up the jail phone. "They did it to Wesley Haynes, now they are doing it to me." He continues.

North Terrace's inmates continually make a mockery of him and have no qualms for expressing their views openly.

"Somebody else is eating your chocolate ice cream while you incarcerate Mr. Lover, Lover..."

Says Son of Judah.

"Your wife owes me money... lots! I need to get paid in full."

Says Hybels.

All this is not only news, real or fabricated but salt in the wound as far as Gregg is concerned. Ever since Hybels pissed on his bed, in Gregg's eyes most of what he says comes through one ear and goes out through the other.

Additionally, it has been rumored among his fellow inmates that his wife was dealing drugs in South Beach at the time of the accident. Even so, there was no evidence to link her to any substance transfer.

Gregg on the other hand tries as much as he can to ignore them but couldn't. He subsequently resorts to a solitude lifestyle. Daily he washes his face, anoint his head, and survives on liquids in search of redemption. So painful...there's not even a song he can spit.

IN JAMAICA as well as other islands in the Caribbean news circulated: the Jamaican police may have played a key role in Milton Rogers' death. Rogers, was known as a shaker and mover, who aligned himself with the late musical tycoon Bill Parsons. With Parsons in the picture, more wounds were now opened up. The media claimed Rogers at one point not only questioned the transparency of Jamaican Law Enforcement but accused that entity of wasting the country's money on the tracking down of Wesley Haynes instead of putting it into education of young people – keeping them off the streets of Kingston.

Rogers never cared much for Sheriff John Brown nor Deputy Ron Charles. The late outspoken uninhibited entrepreneur Milton Rogers had no problems expressing these concerns and more.

"He certainly did not hold his tongue back as far as those matters were concerned."

One Radio talk show host echoed:

"After the Infiniti which was registered to Milton Rogers was discovered in a Jamaican ravine. Peers of Sheriff John Brown and his Deputy Ron Charles pinned the rub out of their two top brass officers on Milton Rogers. Therefore, they sought revenge and rubbed out Rogers in an assassination that will never be forgotten by anyone who ever step inside a courtroom or even watch a LIVE trial on TV."

A version of the theory also suggests that the *people* who assassinated Bill Parsons the late Jamaican music producer and also a close ally of Milton Rogers, paid off Miami Law enforcement to do their dirty work in this tragedy.

Meanwhile, conspiracy theorist continues pointing fingers at Gregg Nichols' in the shooting death of Milton Rogers. They theorize as far as Gregg Nichols' involvement: Wesley Haynes set him up. Haynes knowing: with Milton Rogers out of the picture, the Haynes' Empire would turn into an instant monopoly. Haynes would automatically become the next Jamaican Mogul controlling the entire music world. Every beat and genre would have the Wesley Haynes' branding, even country music. According to media leaks: it was reported that even the Jamaican government in collaboration with the U.S, England, Holland and Germany wanted to stop this monopoly before it got out of control.

CHAPTER **26**

The trial reconvened inside Judge Reuben Melendez's courtroom. The court heard testimonies from two court officers, Daniel Edwards and Errol Clarke.

Daniel Edwards claimed he was situated at the rear of the courtroom and to the right of Quentin Daley. According to Edwards: Gregg Nichols emerged out of the struggle with Daley and allegedly holding on to court officer Quentin Daley's gun.

After the bullet was discharged, Edwards was the first court officer to arrive at the scene. He landed immediately behind detectives Paul Stevens and Mike Jones.

Edwards basically stated to the defense: he saw both men fighting over the gun after Milton Rogers was gunned down. According to Edwards, his main concern was who next is going to get shot. So he rushed to the scene with his gun pointed and demanded:

"Drop the gun! By then the two detectives were already forerunners making the same demands of Nichols.

Edwards claimed by the time he was three feet away from the apparent shooter, the detectives were putting handcuffs on Nichols. The gun was thrown to the ground and kicked aside after failed attempts by Nichols to discharge any additional rounds at this point.

Errol Clarke, on the other hand, when cross-examined by Davis, testified: he was on the right side of the room during the shooting of Rogers. By the time he arrived where Daley and Nichols were struggling for the gun, Nichols was already being handcuffed by the two detectives. So Edwards arrived on the scene moments before Clarke did.

Sebastian Davis further asked: Why it took Clarke so long to arrive at the rear of the court room seeing he had a clear path from the front of the room and only two corners to navigate on the path he chose?

Clarke looking at the location in the courtroom from where the bullet emerged stated:

"I hesitated because I was coming in the direction from whence the bullet which killed Rogers was discharged. If I moved straight ahead, other bullets could have cut me down from straight ahead as I approached the zone of conflict. It was a calculated gut decision I had to make."

The defense then asked Clarke if he was fearful of being shot when he too was armed with a Glock 38. To which he responded:

"It all happened so fast. My thought was what if I removed my gun from its holster and someone grabbed it from me they could have embarked on a shooting spree."

THERE WAS A CHUCKLE from inside the defense's camp earlier during Connolly's cross-examination of Clarke. The DA asked the witness if he had ever seen this before inside a courtroom. To which Clarke jokingly responded: "Never before in my life. Not even in the movies!"

CHAPTER 27

The court next hears testimony from Claude Jefferson, the coroner right after lunch. DA Mark Connolly is profiled at the lectern eager to get on with the trial.

"Mr. Jefferson, from where did you attain your coroner's degree?"

Asks Connolly.

"UCLA School of medicine."

He responds.

"I see. How long have you been performing duties as
a coroner?"
Asks the DA.
"I moved to Miami right after school. It has been a few
months' shy of twelve years."
Says Jefferson.
"Thank you. I've noticed you've been involved in
several high profile cases prior, and that your findings
seem to be very accurate."
Sebastian Davis objects and yells:
"Leading!"
Judge Melendez sustains the objection.
"I am looking at the more than two dozen cases
you've testified in. The record indicates: you have
always been able to support your findings."
"I believe in professionalism. Thank you."
Says Jefferson.
"Who performed the autopsy on Milton Rogers?"
Asks Connolly.
"I did."
"Mr. Jefferson, please educate the court regarding
your findings."
"Mr. Rogers died from a single gunshot wound to his
right side just below his rib-cage. The bullet
penetrated and lodged in his spine."
"How soon after being shot did the victim die?"
Asks Connolly.
"Rogers died on the spot in less than five minutes."

"Was there an inscription on the bullet, and if so whose name was etched on it?"

"Yes. There was, the name Milton Rogers."

Says Jefferson.

"Do you think the victim could have survived?"

"That's possible but with that much damage to this spine he could have been crippled for life."

Says Jefferson.

"Thank you Mr. Jefferson. No further questions."

Sebastian Davis steps up and begins his questioning of the coroner. Among several leading questions without objections from the prosecution, he asked Mr. Jefferson if it was possible to determine the distance from which the bullet was discharged.

Mr. Jefferson stated about 50 feet, the distance of at least one New York MTA train length, which is approximately the length of the court room.

The defense had no further questions. As a result, Judge Melendez set continuation of the trial for the next afternoon.

Ramblings continued as attendees made their exits.

CHAPTER **28**

Not only did Wesley Haynes and Britney Haynes return to Miami from their trip to Paris but Deja's status was upgraded to satisfactory, and released from the hospital. The media, upon announcing Deja's release also claimed the bullet which struck her was a .45 and fired from a .38 45 GAP the same make and model registered to the Miami courthouse and assigned to Officer Quentin Daley.

This bullet went through the upper biceps in her left arm.

One stalker claimed Deja was seen walking in the park on Sunday morning with her two daughters.

That prowler also claimed a well-wisher noticing them in the park, yelled out: "Deja, we love you!" It was said: the artist smiled in recognition of the intentional get-well sentiment. Her daughters also shared in.

HEARINGS IN THE CASE continued on that Monday afternoon. The first afternoon commencement session since the trial began almost two weeks ago.

Even so, the courtroom staff was seen shuffling back and forth, signs of unpreparedness for the afternoon's court proceedings. Even the Judge arrived a few minutes late behind his bench.

Other signs of unrest were also visible, not only inside the jury box but among courtroom attendees as well.

The Bailiff hands a one-page document to Melendez. The Judge puts on his horned rimmed glasses after cleaning the lens carefully to rid of any residue. He then peruses through the page carefully.

"This could be an extended evening if necessary. I just wanted to make every one aware." He says as he sits back in his chair. The court announcer picks up his cue of readiness. She calls Britney Haynes to the witness stand. Some applause accompanies the artist. It seems like many had forgotten the rules of the courtroom and indulged in an extended applause. Britney accepted their sentiment with a modest smile.

However, Melendez quickly called the court to order after glancing at the clock on the rear wall of the courtroom, accompanied by yet another strike of the gavel and a candid look on his face.

Gregg Nichols, in recognition turns around and gives thumbs up to his biggest client and great friend Wesley Haynes, who is encircled by his lawyer Collin Mattes and manager Mr. Singh. The trio, *freshly attired* as if they went shopping with stylists in Paris, acknowledges Gregg Nichols. Wesley returns in kind. They are present at a time when Gregg really needed a boost.

Britney Haynes takes the oath after which DA Mark Connolly begins cross-examination.

"Mrs. Haynes, good afternoon."

Says Connolly with a slight amount of apology in his voice.

To which Britney responds with glee.

"Mrs. Haynes these series of events must be very troubling. I assume."

"They are. For yet another time we are dragged into this debacle."

"The judicature has to do what it must do Mrs. Haynes."

Deja is present in the courtroom and with her arm in a sling shakes her head in disagreement regarding the DA's statement.

"No. It's the system!" Deja says.

"Mrs. Nichols, I am warning you."

Says the Judge.

"Please tell the court about your relationship with the defendant Gregg Nichols."

"I first met Deja Nichols over a year ago when my husband and I were at a low point of our lives and our musical career. More accurately we were about to break up. She introduced me to her ex-boss, Mr. Beckles. Who, at the time was a basement music producer. Deja was very influential in moving our single hit song to a Grammy contender, and eventually a win.

When we met in the park that day, I had no idea all of this would materialize. She later introduced us to her husband Gregg. How I wished Wesley could adopt some of Gregg's humble qualities."

Wesley sitting multiple rows from the front smilingly leans forward in a zinging posture. Britney perks.

Meanwhile, Deja tears up. Large segments of tears run down her blushed cheeks. After that pause Britney continues.

"Gregg took over the business from his boss who was blind and experiencing deteriorating illness. Our second song became a big hit mainly because of their efforts. They are not only associates but we consider them close friends."

Deja dries her tears, clutching onto Gregg's left arm.

Inside the jury box Jurors take copious notes.

The Judge loosens his tie and demands a recess after witnessing Deja's tears trickle down and fall onto the courtroom floor.

CHAPTER 29

District Attorney Mark Connolly visually connects with jurors before proceeding.

"Mrs. Haynes, you were inside the courtroom when Milton Rogers was gunned down. Were you not?"

"I was. My husband and I were the first to arrive as he fell backwards off that witness stand."

"Did you see Gregg Nichols shoot Milton Rogers?"

Asks Connolly

"No. I did not."

Says Britney

"Did he tell you he shot Milton Rogers for fame or an inheritance of his estate?"

Asks Connolly.

"He did not. Gregg is not that kind of person."

Says Britney.

"Mrs. Haynes, are you also one of the beneficiaries to Milton Rogers' estate?"

Attorney Sebastian Davis objects.

Judge Melendez sustains the objection.

"You may answer the question."

Says Connolly.

"I am not a beneficiary."

Replies Britney Haynes.

"Mrs. Haynes, in regards to your friend Deja Nichols: Do you know her by an alias or what some may call an aka?"

"I do."

"And what's that?"

Asks Connolly.

"Grace!"

"Do you know her by any other aliases?"

"No. I don't."

Responds Britney.

"And the defendant Gregg Nichols?"

Asks Connolly.

"I only know him as Gregg."

Says Britney.

"No further questions, your honor."

Says Connolly.

The Judge eyes the clock.

After a pause in the trial's proceedings:

"Your witness counselor."

Says Melendez.

Sebastian Davis, after greeting Britney compliments her for a unique display of courage in a back to back trial and in the same courtroom.

Britney sobs continuously like a running stream.

The Judge suggested Britney take a minute or two before continuing her testimony as she remains engulfed in tears.

"I am fine."

Says Britney.

Gregg Nichols focuses on Deja now engulfed in the secondary courtroom drama – a tear jerking episode accompanied by sobs of suffering.

"Oppression Never Done!"

Yells Gregg Nichols.

Court officers amble towards the section of the room where those three words echoed.

"Silence in court!"

Says Melendez.

Residual murmuring continues.

"Let's clear out the courtroom."

Summons Melendez.

Court officers pounce and subsequently the courtroom empties out.

CHAPTER 30

The trial reconvenes after yet another prolonged unscheduled intermission. A logistics and calm down interruption, to say the least or better yet: A long time out. An intermission much needed to get everyone back on cue.

Defense attorney Sebastian Davis continues.

"Mrs. Haynes, please tell this court about your relationship with the victim Milton Rogers."

"Milton Rogers gave Wesley and me our first job when we moved from Mandeville to Kingston. He took us under his wings, so to speak. Rogers was a great friend and mentor to Wesley. He would always say to Wesley: '*The heights by great men reached and kept were not attained by sudden flight, but they, while their companions slept, were toiling upward in the night.*' Wesley took that statement to heart. It seemed to have entered every fiber of his being. It became his mantra. We would always be grateful to Mr. Milton Rogers."

"I see. Did you or your husband conspire to murder Milton Rogers?"

Asks Sebastian Davis.

"We did not. We loved Mr. Rogers; he had done so much for us. We would never entertain an ungrateful thought towards him. Milton Rogers paved the way for Wesley and Me."

Responds Britney.

"Do you know of anyone who did?"

Asks Davis.

"No. I do not."

"Mrs. Haynes, if you were asked to etch the epitaph on Milton Rogers' tombstone what would you write?"

Britney thinks for a moment. She breathes before answering.

"Here lies a man who gave and gave until there was nothing else to give to the advancement of international music."

Says the multiple Grammy winner, Britney Haynes.

"Thank you Mrs. Haynes. No further questions."

"Mrs. Haynes you may step down."

Says Melendez.

At this point Britney Haynes is once again engulfed in tears.

Two aids accompanied by Wesley Haynes emerge and escorts Britney outside the courtroom. Wesley's lawyer and manager follow in tow.

Deja reflects and once again tears up. Gregg puts his arm around her and consoles.

Melendez call for yet another post-tear-jerking-recess. Many believed that the unusual amounts of tears in the courtroom had a traumatic effect on the Judge.

CHAPTER 31

After the break, DA Mark Connolly approaches the lectern. Ballistics expert Lloyd Matthews is on the witness stand. Connolly begins cross-examination.

"Mr. Matthews, the record states you are from the island of Jamaica and was recently transferred to the Ballistics department here in Miami. Is that correct?"

"That's correct."

Says Matthews.

"What's the tenure of your career?"

"Ten years and counting…"

"Mr. Matthews, you were inside this courtroom on Valentine's Day when Milton Rogers was shot. Were you not?"

"I was."

"Would you say that was coincidental on your part?"

"Yes. It was."

Responds Matthews.

"Tell the court what you saw."

"I saw Rogers react to being shot after a single round of gunfire. I then turned around, looking to see where that shot originated. My eyes saw and locked in on two men struggling over a gun. I found out later the wrestlers were Gregg Nichols and Quentin Daley."

"Did you ask to be assigned to this case?"

"I did not. They sought me out."

"Based on your findings, what type of gun was used in the shooting death of Milton Rogers?"

"It was a Glock 38."

"Have you worked on other cases where the type of gun in question was used?"

"Objection!"

Shouts Sebastian Davis.

"Objection overruled."

Says Melendez adjusting his glasses.

Mr. Matthews, I cite in the Who Shot the Sheriff? Case
vs Wesley Haynes, you testified: three replicas of
Glock 38s were used. Isn't that so?"

"I did."

"You testified earlier, one bullet was fired in that
incident on Valentine's Day, inside this courtroom.

"I did."

"Based on your findings, how many bullets remained
inside the gun's magazine after that fatal shot was
fired?"

"The gun was empty."

"What's the capacity of a Glock 38 magazine?"

"Eight rounds."

"How many bullets were recovered from the victim's
body?"

"One bullet."

Based on your findings, how many bullets were
discharged from the gun?"

"One single bullet."

Replied Matthews.

"What test did your lab perform to determine the
bullet matched the gun recovered at the crime scene?"
Asks Connolly.

"Our regular procedure was once again followed. A
bullet from that gun was fired into a tank filled with
water. After that bullet was recovered, it was viewed
under a microscope and determined a match."

"Mr. Matthews, to your knowledge were there any
additional guns used in that shooting incident?"

"It is clear there was one gun. One bullet with its shell residue which displayed the name *Milton Rogers* on it."

Responds Matthews.

"Was the name etched in caps or lower case?"

"It was etched in sentence case and italicized."

The Bailiff presents a package. Matthews opens it, removes a slide and places it into the projector. The fragment shell casing is visible. He zooms in and shows a close-up of the etched shell. "This is exhibit number two."

Says Mathews and returns to the witness stand.

"Were there fingerprints on the gun and whose?"

Asks Connolly.

"There were prints lifted for Quentin Daley and Gregg Nichols and Errol Clarke."

"Were any of these prints widely distributed on the Glock 38?"

"Yes, in and around the trigger area. I must say Gregg Nichols prints dominated the entire gun, as well as inside the gun's magazine."

"Objection. Your honor, I move to strike the last sentence."

Says Sebastian Davis.

"Objection overruled."

Says Melendez.

"So basically, the defendant had maximum control of the weapon as indicated by a dominance of his fingerprints inside and out?"

Says Connolly.

"That is a given."

Responds Matthews.

"What percentage of Errol Clarke's fingerprints was found on the gun?"

"A small percentage."

"How small?"

Asks Connolly.

"At least 20%."

Responds Matthews.

"What percentage for Quentin Daley?"

"At least 30%."

Says Matthews.

"So, that means the defendant, Gregg Nichols' fingerprints dominated with a whopping 50%?"

"Yes. I would say that..."

"Objection! Move to strike."

Says Davis.

"Overruled."

Says Melendez.

"Based upon your findings Mr. Matthews: did the defendant load or reload the gun?"

"That is possible. The location of his prints on that gun would suggest he did."

Says Matthews.

"Thank you Mr. Matthews. No further questions."

Says Connolly.

The DA walks back to his seat.

On the witness stand Ballistics expert Lloyd Matthews
stays put.

CHAPTER 32

Sebastian Davis approaches with strides of determination and focus. He must be going for the jugular that of Lloyd Matthews' - Gregg reasons.

Restlessness exudes from within the Jury Box. Poise resounds on the face of Gregg Nichols. Deja's face shows genuine support.

"Mr. Matthews, you testified earlier, you were inside the courtroom when Milton Rogers was gunned down. Is that correct?"

"It is correct."

Says Matthews.

"Why were you there at that time?"

"I had just finished testifying in the case vs Wesley Haynes and seeing Rogers was going to be the last witness in the case I wanted to witness his testimony. Thoughts of leaving entered my mind but I decided to stay."

"So, did you witness the shooting of Milton Rogers?"

"No. As I explained I heard a round of gunshots and saw Milton Rogers fall backwards on the witness stand, holding his chest."

"You did not? Didn't you see the defendant Gregg Nichols shoot and kill Milton Rogers?"

Asks Davis.

"You are putting words in my mouth. I am here to testify about my ballistics findings as an expert. From my vantage point I did not see who fired the fatal round. However, when I turned around, I saw Quentin and Nichols fighting for control of the gun. I must say: based on y findings Nichols' finger prints dominated the weapon."

Says Matthews.

"I was of the opinion you saw everything."

Says Sebastian Davis.

Connolly is standing at this point but gracefully sits back down.

Attorney Davis continues.

"Expert! Didn't your findings err in the case Wesley Haynes vs Sheriff John Brown and Deputy Ron Charles?"

"Err?"

Asks Lloyd Matthews.

"Yes... Err. For use of a better word slip up, or in error?"

"The court granted permission to my department to further investigate the bullets which shot the Sheriff and his Deputy. I provided them with those results per their request."

"So as an expert your work is in error sometimes or not definitive or conclusive?"

"I do my job the way I was trained."

Says Matthews.

"So you are trained to err, or slip up every now and then in order to manufacture a misleading conviction?"

"That's not how I do my job."

Says Matthews.

"You also testified earlier, it is possible the defendant loaded or reloaded the gun."

"I did."

"Where did he put the bullet or bullets he removed from the gun's magazine? They were not found on his person."

"Hypothetically, he could have swallowed them."
Says Matthews.
"All eight bullets were swallowed without a glass of water?"
Asks Sebastian Davis.
"I don't know how many rounds was present inside the gun before Rogers was shot."
Says Matthews.
"Did he pass any bullets out in his stool?"
Asks Davis.
"We don't know that."
Says Matthews.
"Did anyone check?"
Asks Attorney Davis.
The courtroom erupts with laughter. The striking of the gavel restores some sense of order.
"No one did. Several days had passed before remains of that fatal bullet was transported to me by the coroner's office. Nichols had already been locked up for several days. We had no way of knowing. Or else someone could have monitored his feces."
Says Matthews.
"In addition to the fingerprints of the defendant Gregg Nichols and court officer Quentin Daley, were there other prints lifted from that gun?"
"Yes."
Says Matthews.
"Whose?"
Asks Davis.

"Court Officer Errol Clarke."

Says Matthews.

"Interesting ... so he too was in contact with that gun. Yet, he didn't pull the trigger. Your honor, no further questions."

Says Sebastian Davis stares in the vicinity of the Jury box before returning to his seat.

CHAPTER 33

Severe weightiness emerge from lawful psychoanalysts as to why court officer Errol Clarke's fingerprints were found on the gun which shot Milton Rogers. Now the nucleus of media related debates began filtering into the trial. Many feared the jury would become polluted with outside influence.

It is a given, Clarke didn't say too much in his testimony. However, many legal experts felt there was more to be said from the co-worker of Quentin Daley, the officiating partner to the possible gunman, even though he might have been accused, yet not officially charged.

Clarke's prints on the gun was unsettling as many legal experts try to unravel the case outside the courtroom.

Meanwhile, inside Judge Melendez's courtroom, as if it was an act of fate, Errol Clarke was recalled to the witness stand. After what seemed like a swift reading of the oath, cross-examination began. DA Mark Connolly proceeds to the lectern.

"Mr. Clarke, did you load or reload your co-worker's gun prior to the trial on Valentine's Day?"

"No. I did not. I saw him load that gun himself."

Says Errol Clarke.

"How many bullets did he load into that gun's magazine?"

"One bullet."

"Didn't it concern you that your co-worker was carrying a gun with only one bullet inside its magazine?"

"I don't check my co-workers' weapon to determine how many rounds they have loaded inside."

Says Clarke.

"Were there other bullets inside that gun?"

Asks Connolly.

"I really don't know."
Says Clarke.
"No further questions."
Says Connolly.

ATTORNEY SEBASTIAN DAVIS steps into the witnesses' *paint* attempting to score a few points.
"Mr. Clarke in your testimony earlier, you stated you had never seen any incident in the courtroom like the Roger's shooting. Were you implying an incident of such magnitude had to be properly executed?"
"It had to be well planned."
Says Clarke.
"So you concur it had to have been well planned?"
"Yes. Proper planning is the foundation of any well executed venture."
Says Clarke.
"Did you share the same dressing room with Officer Daley on the day Milton Rogers was shot?"
Clarke hesitates.
"Did you Mr. Clarke?"
"I did."
"Your fingerprints were found on his gun. That same gun which took the life of Milton Rogers. What was your intent?"
"We carry the same guns of the same make and model. A Glock 38 gray in color is a Glock 38 gray in color. It is quite possible I took up his gun by mistake while getting ready for the trial."

Clarke states.

"By mistake?"

Asks Sebastian Davis.

"So, did you touch his gun or did you tamper with his gun while it was inside the shared dressing room?"

"I don't recall touching his gun. If I did it was by accident."

"Did you open his gun and reloaded it?"

"I did not. If it happened that was a mistake."

"A mistake to reload?"

"I did not. As I said, I don't recall handling his gun. If I did it was an unconscious mistake."

"Unconscious? Mr. Clarke did your unconscious decision also limit you from rushing through the center aisle in the court room to the aid of your fellow officer while he tried to recapture his gun?"

"I don't understand."

Says Clarke.

"You said in previous testimony: Instead of going through the center aisle you went left, turn the corner and headed towards the rear of the courtroom."

"Yes. That is what happened."

"Why did you choose the longer route instead of the shorter and more direct one? Were you trained to wait or to respond?"

"I made an instinctual decision."

Says Clarke.

"Just like the one you did when you tampered with your co-worker's weapon. Your honor, I have no further questions."

CHAPTER 34

There were no more eyewitnesses called in the case. It seemed as though that was it for all the testifying in this case. The court took an extended recess.

It was widely distributed: Gregg Nichols shot Milton Rogers. Even if many flaunted with the epiphany or the conspiracy theory: Rogers shot John Brown and his Deputy Ron Charles, now Rogers was also snuffed out. As far as it seemed, Gregg Nichols was their man; in their eyes he was guilty until proven innocent. If he is not acquitted, he could fry in Florida's electric chair or on a lesser charge be locked away for life if eventually convicted.

However, it was also heavily debated among legal experts: others could have been responsible for that double homicide in which Wesley Haynes was found not guilty. That same entity could have also orchestrated the Milton Rogers' ambush. Even if no one claimed responsibility for the Mogul's death.

When the trial resumed, Melendez asked Connolly to present his closing statements.

DA Mark Connolly rose to the occasion. He straightened his tie, unbuttoned his jacket, and greeted the judge and then 12 jurors with a broad smile. To which they responded in kind but modestly. His decorum was like a fresh beginning in the trial which now lasted more than a month since jury selection.

"Your honor, jurors, other court attendees. It has be a long and tiring six weeks hearing testimonies and weighing through this preponderance of evidence. I am sure you're like me wanting to put this whole matter to rest. On Valentine's Day last year, Jamaican Mogul Milton Rogers was gunned down while testifying inside this courtroom. Some saw Milton Rogers shoot Rogers after which he engaged in a struggle for the court officer's gun. Although some may argue it wasn't the defendant Gregg Nichols who fired that fatal shot which killed Milton Rogers. There's preponderance of evidence stacked up against Gregg Nichols. It is clear; based on the testimonies given, he had multiple motives for killing Rogers, even though the defense may beg to differ.

Gregg Nichols could have been in search of fame.

By shooting the Jamaican Mogul he would join the club of *Whodunits Murderers* like the Lee Harvey Oswald's' of the world.

Nichols could have shot Rogers in order to cover up information in the death of Sheriff John Brown and his Deputy Ron Charles.

Wesley Haynes was Nichols' close friend. Chances are Nichols was afraid Rogers would disclose relevant information to support a Haynes' guilty verdict. So he snuffed out Rogers.

Knowingly that Rogers and Haynes had strong financial ties.

Wanting to replace Rogers in the musical chain could have been paramount, so he snuffed out Milton Rogers.

Those are strong and possible motives for shooting Rogers inside that courtroom.

To think anyone else could have been responsible: is nothing but ludicrous.

Gregg Nichols is guilty for shooting Milton Rogers as the evidence have shown.

Members of the jury it's your responsibility to deliver justice in this case. Allowing a guilty man to walk free would be forever on your conscience if you do not convict him. We the prosecution rests."
Multiple eyes are fixated on the defendant while DA Mark Connolly strolls across the front of the courtroom and takes his pew.

CHAPTER 35

M elendez wasted no time calling on defense lawyer Sebastian Davis. With his chest stuck out Davis approached the jury box and engages them.

"Ladies and gentlemen of the jury. In a trial which has lasted almost two months. It is apparent the gunman who shot and killed Milton Rogers isn't a first time offender. I don't believe my client Gregg

Nichols shot and killed Rogers. I believe this assassination style killing was not only well orchestrated but a collaborated effort.

Case in point: Court officer Errol Clarke's fingerprints were lifted from the gun belonging to his co-worker officer Quentin Daley. My question to you is: Why? Why would someone else fingerprints appear on a gun which he is not permitted to have in his possession?

Quentin Daley the court officer, was permitted to carry that gun to protect the judge, jury, law enforcement personnel as well as other courtroom attendees. Why was there only one bullet inside that gun's magazine? Why wasn't that gun fully loaded by this court officer? Who supplied that one bullet? Is still a mystery. Did it come through osmosis, divine providence or some heartless killer who wants to see my client convicted for a crime he did not commit?

If Gregg Nichols detached the other seven ammunitions, what did he do with them? No bullets were recovered inside the courtroom nor on his person. Some might argue: Nichols could have swallowed the bullets. It takes time to gulp one horse pill with water, much less without water. The bullets used in that Glock are much grander than horse pills. If it takes at least five seconds to swallow a bullet with water. We can assume it would take three times that time to swallow one without water. It would therefore take 105 seconds to swallow all seven bullets without breathing after each ingestion.

Detectives Jones and Stevens present inside the courtroom and seated a few rows away. They would have gotten to Nichols before he had an opportunity to discharge that fatal bullet.

The bullet which took Rogers life had Rogers' name etched on it according to the ballistics report. Let's say the gun was fully loaded with eight bullets. Let's say Nichols removed the other seven bullets, how did he know which bullet had Milton Rogers' name etched on it?

Additionally, if Nichols had to reload Quentin Daley's gun with a bullet which he brought with him inside the courtroom through tight security, and there were 8 bullets inside that gun prior, that's an extra 15 seconds elapse to swallow another bullet. Thus, making it 120 seconds, which the last time I checked equals 2 full minutes. So did Nichols swallow all those bullets in 2 minutes and then pulled the trigger? In essence 4 thirty second commercials would have been aired before he pulled that trigger.

Let's say it took him 1 minute to tackle court officer Daley, and 15 seconds to open the gun's magazine and remove eight bullets, 2 minutes to swallow them. Then let's say it took him 15 seconds to load the etched – fatal bullet, close the gun's magazine, get the perfect aim and then shoot Rogers. That is 3 and1/2 minutes. A total of seven 30 seconds commercials aired since he confronted Quentin, the court officer to the time the fatal bullet was discharged. I don't but that and neither do you. It doesn't add up.

If Nichols really loaded that gun with one bullet, then it is evident the gun was empty. Which means that court officer Daley was unarmed during a high profile case. That crime should be punishable by law.

We must ask ourselves: Was the Rogers' shooting a collaborative effort between Errol Clarke, Marcus Davis and Quentin Daley?

Marcus Davis testified he had a long lasting beef with Wesley Haynes and Milton Rogers over a shipment of undelivered marijuana.

Additionally, Marcus Davis had plans to join the witness protection program so he could shield himself from any crime. The fact remains: Did Marcus Davis collaborate with court officer's Clarke and Daley to eliminate the Jamaican Mogul, Milton Rogers inside the courtroom?

All these questions we must ask ourselves. I do not believe the defendant Gregg Nichols shot Milton Rogers. Time and Time again, I've seen men go to prison for a crime they did not commit. This has to stop. This trial is our opportunity to stop this trend. My client is a decent citizen who wishes to continue living a fulfilled life. Let him go so he can do just that."

Sebastian Davis moved full circle and winds up directly in-front of the jury box tapping on their heart doors.

"I look forward to your non guilty verdict in regards to my client."

Sebastian Davis walks back to his seat to thumbs up from Gregg Nichols.

Judge Melendez announced the jury will deliberate and return with a verdict in three days. The agitated courtroom attendees file out.

CHAPTER 36

eturning to North Terrace, it was Gregg Nichols' objective to get some much needed R and R. With deliberation already underway he couldn't wait to lay his head down and rid his mind of the hearing of testimonies ordeal. His desire was to be free once again, living the life he always envisioned that of an artist and entrepreneur. Even so, one more uncertainty beckoned – the verdict.

That night at North Terrace oblivious to Gregg
Nichols, his neighbors concocted a plot to avenge him.
They had watched that day's proceedings in the trial
via the prison's flat screen TV hitched high above their
heads inside the recreation room. Evidently had been
well informed regarding the current status of the
proceedings.

While Nichols amble towards his cell, he felt the hand
of someone stroking his neck and shoulders. As he
turned around he came face to face with Hybels his
upstairs neighbor, who maliciously sent urine down
onto his bed on his first night at North Terrace.

"What is your problem?" He ask Hybels.

Smilingly Hybels states:

"I want to get you off my calendar. One big check
mark."

Coming at Hybels with a clenched fist, Nichols asks:
"You do? Really?"

"You have been sitting far too long on my - *to do list*.
It's time to check you."

Responds Hybels.

Nichols punches him hard in the face.

Hybels retaliates, favoring his non-functioning left
arm. It has been recent news: Hybels left arm was
paralyzed after his prolonged use of contaminated
methamphetamine.

Both inmates go at it exchanging vicious punches.

The fight escalates with Gregg Nichols gaining the upper hand. How Hybels wished there was a bell. None chimed and no referee interceded.

The duel continues for several minutes until Hybels is sent to the ground twirling with a straight kick from Gregg Nichols.

"I am sorry man."

Says Hybels.

Son of Judah, witnessing those final moments of the bout between Hybels and Nichols grabs the mop stick from the janitor who is trying to access his hand held radio to usher in backup. Moving towards Nichols he swats the janitor across his neck with the mop. The fabric portion of the mop severs from the stick.

Before closing in on Gregg Nichols, Son of Judah breaks the stick into two halves, and comes swinging at Nichols. It doesn't take long, Nichols disarms him.

Hybels gets back up and charges at Gregg Nichols. Gregg administers two quick kicks into Hybels stomach. Hybels gets back up and charges at Nichols. Another kick plants him to the ground. Now he is badly hurt and favors that other arm.

Son of Judah now back on his feet comes charging and swinging at Gregg. They pursue each other aggressively. Son of Judah finally puts Gregg to the pavement locked into a clinch with the arm behind his back. Hybels emerges to even the score.

Gregg pries himself out of the clinch and seizes the opportunity to administer blows to Son of Judah's body sending him reeling to the ground. Spectating inmates yell from their cells: "Fight! Martyrdom! Dead meat! As well as other catchwords for a grotesque bloodbath.

Kyle Chang as high as a kite emerges from out of nowhere and immediately confronts Nichols, displaying multiple eagle-like karate moves: First some eagle moves and then the snake. Nichols ineptness does not match up with Chang's adeptness. Inmates chant louder in favor of Chang.

"Give him the Chinese move. Bruce Lee and all. Flying tiger and hide that dragon. Bite him like a snake and claw him like an eagle."

Nichols is on the ground as a result and coughing up blood accompanied by droplets of the same, emitting from his face and upper body. As a result of some viscous clawing administered by Chang and directly towards his throat.

The two officers Knowles and Thomas springing onto the scene. Nichols is still down. No one counts to ten. Chang tries to get away. They trap Chang before he does. Officers retrieve water hose from now standing janitor and hose down both Chang and Nichols.

Son of Judah and Hybels are subsequently carried away from the scene on gurneys. Chang and Nichols spend that night in the holes.

CHAPTER 37

B ack inside the courtroom the next morning. It seems as if everyone is waiting for the ball to drop, so to speak. Gregg Nichols enters the courtroom through that side door just like he did at the beginning of the trial. Except for this time his left arm is in a sling and multiple concussions saturate his face and head.

The aura inside the courtroom has transformed since his entry. No late breaking news announced the cause of the defendant's injury.

Consequently, many believed it was all a hoax; an attempt to sway some sympathy in Nichols' direction. Even so, Gregg Nichols appeared to be in severe pain and discomfort.

Defense lawyer Sebastian Davis walks in, leaving ample space between himself and Nichols. On the other side Deja Nichols carefully mops her husband's brow with a rag now soaked with his blood, sweat and tears.

Judge Melendez strikes the gavel in readiness. "Let me remind this court that our duty here today is to obtain a verdict from the jury and nothing else."

Judge Melendez had been briefed earlier by prison officials at North Terrace regarding the altercation between Gregg Nichols and three other inmates.

However, the Judge was hesitant to call off the trial, for fear the Jury with too much time off might toss some pollution into the verdict.

"Is the foreperson ready?" Melendez asks.

"Yes your honor."

The six foot plus Caucasian man replies.

"Wait one moment."

Says Melendez as he checks to make sure the courtroom has been adequately staffed with court officers. Noticing one of the officers engaged in conversation with a Miami Police officer, he addresses:

"Gentlemen this court is already called to order. Are you ready to proceed?"

The two officers quickly part company.

"Go ahead Mr. Foreman."

Instructs Melendez.

"Your honor during our deliberation we came up with a multiplicity of charges. This might be somewhat unorthodox in a trial but these are the verdicts."

Many heads turn as the last word dropped in its plural state.

The foreman continues: In the shooting death of Milton Rogers, we find the defendant Gregg Nichols not guilty."

The defense section goes ballistic. Deja plants a big kiss on Gregg. He aches from her act of affection but exhibits jubilance. Many attendees begin to file out. However, the foreman is still standing.

Melendez strikes his gavel once again.

"Silence in court!"

He yells and continues.

"The foreperson is still standing, which means we are not yet finished with the court's business."

Those who exited are now returning as if more time is put back on the clock and the score is tied as we go into overtime. You can now hear a pin drop after court attendees take their seats.

"Your honor, on the count of perjury: we find court officer Errol Clarke guilty."

A state of wonderment engulfs the courtroom. Melendez once again strikes his gavel.

"On the count of murder of Milton Rogers, we find court officer Quentin Daley guilty."

The foreperson takes his seat.

Hugs follow on one side of the courtroom.

Gregg Nichols re-injures his left arm as Deja squeezes on him with her injured right arm. "Ouch" Says Gregg as he flinches once in pain. "The truth has been told. Justice has spoken. Free at last!"

Those were the only time he glued that many sentences together during the entire trial.

CHAPTER 38

Three days after the sentencing of Errol Clarke and Quentin Daley, news broke stating not only that Hybels was removed from the hole now with his other hand in a sling as a result of the beating from Nichols. In other related news, sources claimed the Methamphetamine which was responsible for paralyzing Hybels other arm was supplied by Deja Nichols aka Yuki Barnes.

Deja Nichols was subsequently arrested by Miami Police and detained.

Meanwhile, according to sources an elderly man from South Beach followed Deja as she made a drop off of Methamphetamine to a prison officer at the same building across the street where she was shot a month ago. The elderly man had also witnessed the drive by shooting incident in which Deja was shot in the arm, while he was riding in the park.

Following the tip police were led to the 'North Terrace' cell block at the Broward County Prison in Miami. Freddie Knowles, the prison officer made that delivery to Raymond Hybels every time he was brought to the hole.

Police also said Deja Nichols used the aka Yuki Barnes to make her drop offs at the drug depot in South Beach.

Over half a million dollars in contraband money was later discovered in a multiple layered trash bag in an underground manhole at North Terrace leading to Son of Judah's cell.

Medical experts are claiming the Meth supplied by Yuki was contaminated and mixed with a foreign substance. Many inmates including Richard Hybels used the substance provided by Yuki and later wound up with non-functional body parts.

MARCUS DAVIS WAS ALSO ARRESTED hours later in the drive by shooting incident of Deja Nichols aka Yuki Barnes several weeks ago. According to sources multiple shells shot from the same gun which injured the artist were recovered from the crime scene in South Beach.

Additionally, one eyewitness who preferred to be unidentified provided information which led to the arrest of Davis. Police followed that lead which led to them to an abandoned BMW. A collection of reconstructed Glock 38s was also recovered from the trunk of the automobile.

Ballistics findings indicate, seven bullets were fired from the gun found on the front passenger seat. The one bullet which remained inside that gun's magazine had Wesley Haynes' name etched on it.

FLASHBACK ALMOST ONE YEAR AGO:

NIGHT CLUB IN JAMAICA...AUGUST 12th.

Surveillance camera shows Marcus Davis driving away from the parking lot inside a black Infiniti, bearing temporary license tags on that same night and hours before Sheriff John Brown and Ron Charles were gunned down.

About The Author

John A. Andrews hails from the beautiful Islands of St. Vincent and the Grenadines in the Caribbean.

He is a prolific, International Bestselling author whose works include: Rude Buay ... The Unstoppable. A gritty "drug prevention" action thriller which delves into the drug corruption, the deception, the deceit, of the drug epidemic sweeping through Jamaica and up into America. A series of books which many has already dubbed "A Black James Bond Series."

Other works include: The Whodunit Chronicles. Included in this mystery series are titles such as: Who Shot the Sheriff? and A Snitch on Time. The author is also known for his Hard-Boiled detective work in Renegade Cops. His writing portfolio also includes books for teens on success as well as other personal development titles.

Andrews who fantasized with becoming a cop as a little boy studied acting at Lee Strasberg Institute in NYC. He later brought his acting to Hollywood in 1997. He continued honing his acting craft at Van Mar Academy under the tutelage of Ivan Markota, the Star-maker. According to Andrews "The late Ivan Markota didn't just teach acting but he taught the business   of   Hollywood."

John Andrews has since performed in multiple TV campaigns for Nike, AT&T, Hollywood Video, EMC Squared, Compaq Computers, Nasdaq. He appeared in John Q, and Films with Charlie Sheen and other major   stars.

Many see him as a visionary, who, after being denied the rights to a film in 2002, which he badly wanted to remake, decided to would write his own. That rejection triggered his now writing career.

Not many authors are adept at turning their novel into screenplay and vice versa. Andrews prides himself as a part of the elite pact.

Mentored in film by one of Hollywood's top film producers in Mark Burg, John Andrews has seen many films come to the big screen including JOHN Q starring Denzel Washington, and the SAW franchise and others. According to Andrews: "Mark. Burg always invited me on the set, whether film or TV. I did embrace those opportunities. He always kept me in the know and was never reluctant when it came to introducing me to his allies. On set, I learned how to see things through a producer's eyes. One of the gems I picked up from him is that he always came in under budget.

Mr. Andrews is the father of 3 teenage boys, Jonathan, Jefferri and Jamison. Jonathan and Jefferri collaboratively released their first novel in 2013 and are not only turning it into a sequel but co-authored "Who Shot the Sheriff? II.

See more in: HOW I RAISED MYSELF FROM FAILURE TO SUCCESS IN HOLLYWOOD.

Visit: www.JohnAAndrews.com

CO-AUTHORS

Jonathan Winston Andrews was born in Jamaica, New York. He grew up in Sherman Oaks, Los Angeles, California and resides in Bishopville, South

Carolina.

Jonathan is very close with his brothers Jefferri and Jamison and his step-brother Adam Jowers.

Jonathan is co-author of The Macos Adventure novel series.

He loves to play video games, listen to music, and play the piano. He is currently studying Accounting.

Jefferri Andrews was born in Long Island, Nassau County, New York. He has two brothers Jonathan and Jamison. and a step-brother named Adam Jowers.

Jefferri grew up in Sherman Oaks, Los Angeles,

California for eight years and currently resides in Bishopville, South Carolina.

Jefferri is co-author of The Macos Adventure novel series. Jefferri loves to listen to metalcore and post hardcore bands, shop at Hot Topic, make YouTube videos, and read young adult novels.

He gets inspiration for writing from watching teen dramas such as The Fosters, Teen Wolf, and Finding Carter.

.

Check out Upcoming Titles
&
New Releases...

RUDE BUAY ... RETURNS

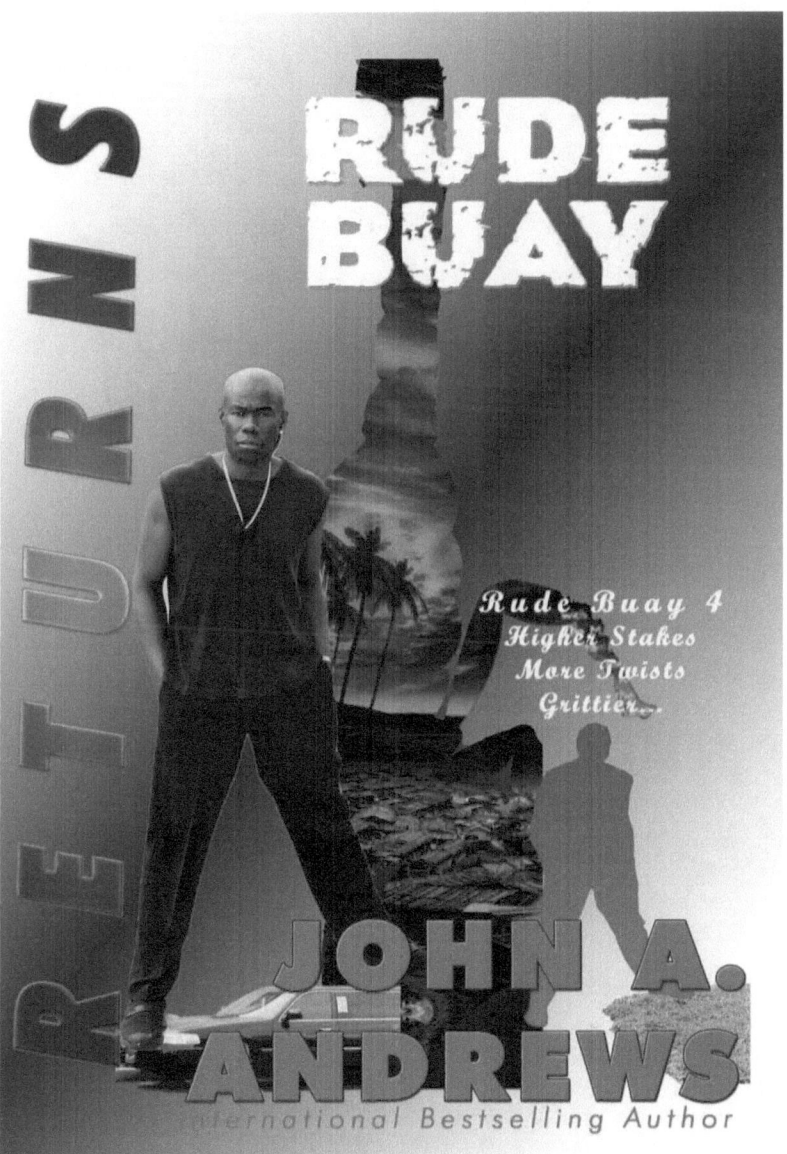

RENEGADE COPS 2

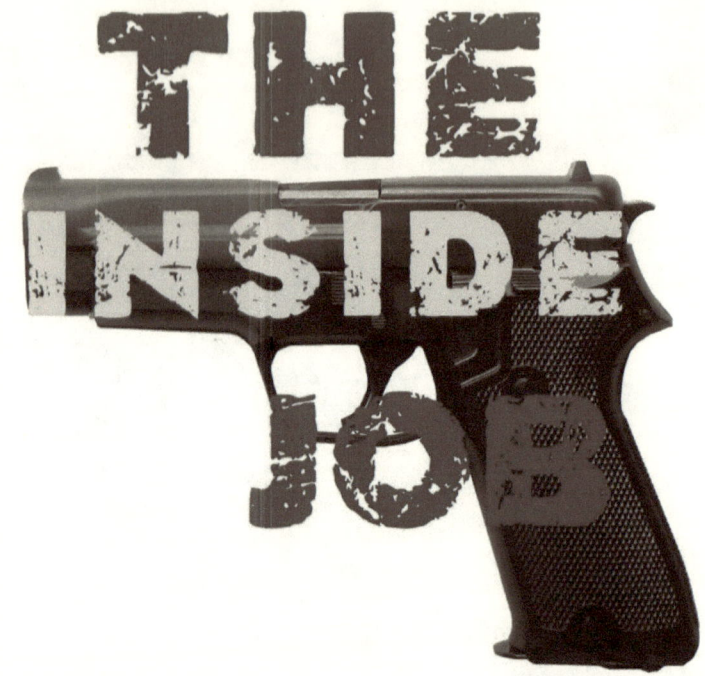

THE INSIDE JOB

RENEGADE COPS 2

JOHN A. ANDREWS

CREATOR OF
THE RUDE BUAY SERIES
&
THE WHODUNIT CHRONICLES

WHO SHOT THE SHERIFF? III

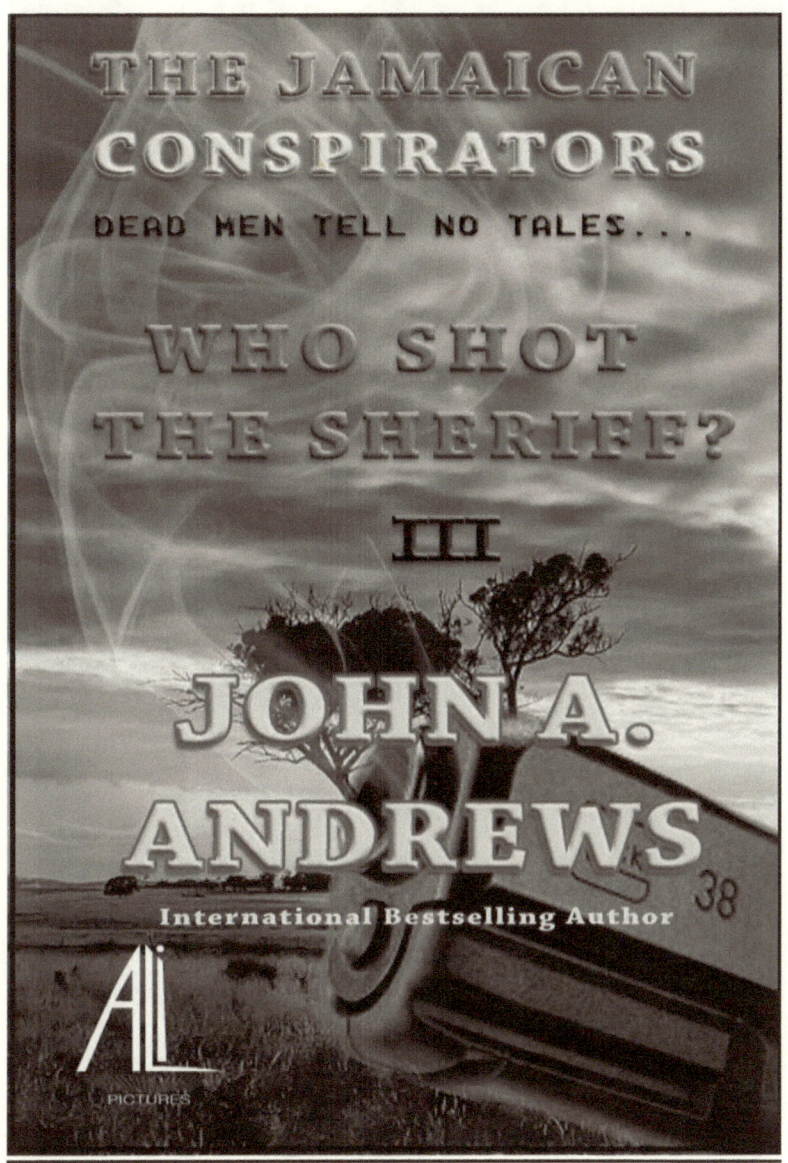

WHO SHOT THE SHERIFF?

RUDE BUAY ... The UNSTOPPABLE

A SNITCH ON TIME

THE MACOS ADVENTURE II

RUDE BUAY ... THE
UNTOUCHABLE

CHICO RUDO ... El INTOCABLE

RUDE BUAY...SHATTERPROOF

RENEGADE COPS

CROSS
ATLANTIC
FIASCO

BLOOD IS THICKER THAN WATER

JOHN A. ANDREWS
RENEGADE COPS
Creator of
The RUDE BUAY Series
&
The WHODUNIT CHRONICLES

HOW I RAISED MYSELF FROM FAILURE TO SUCCESS IN HOLLYWOOD

OTHER RELEASES

HOW I WROTE 8 BOOKS IN ONE YEAR

How I Wrote 8 Books In One Year

JOHN A. ANDREWS

A

Author of

TOTAL COMMITMENT

The Mindset Of Champions

QUOTES UNLIMITED II

DARE TO MAKE A
DIFFERENCE – SUCCESS 101

National Bestselling Author

Dare To Make
A
Difference

SUCCESS 101

JOHN A. ANDREWS

QUOTES UNLIMITED

THE 5 STEPS TO CHANGING YOUR LIFE

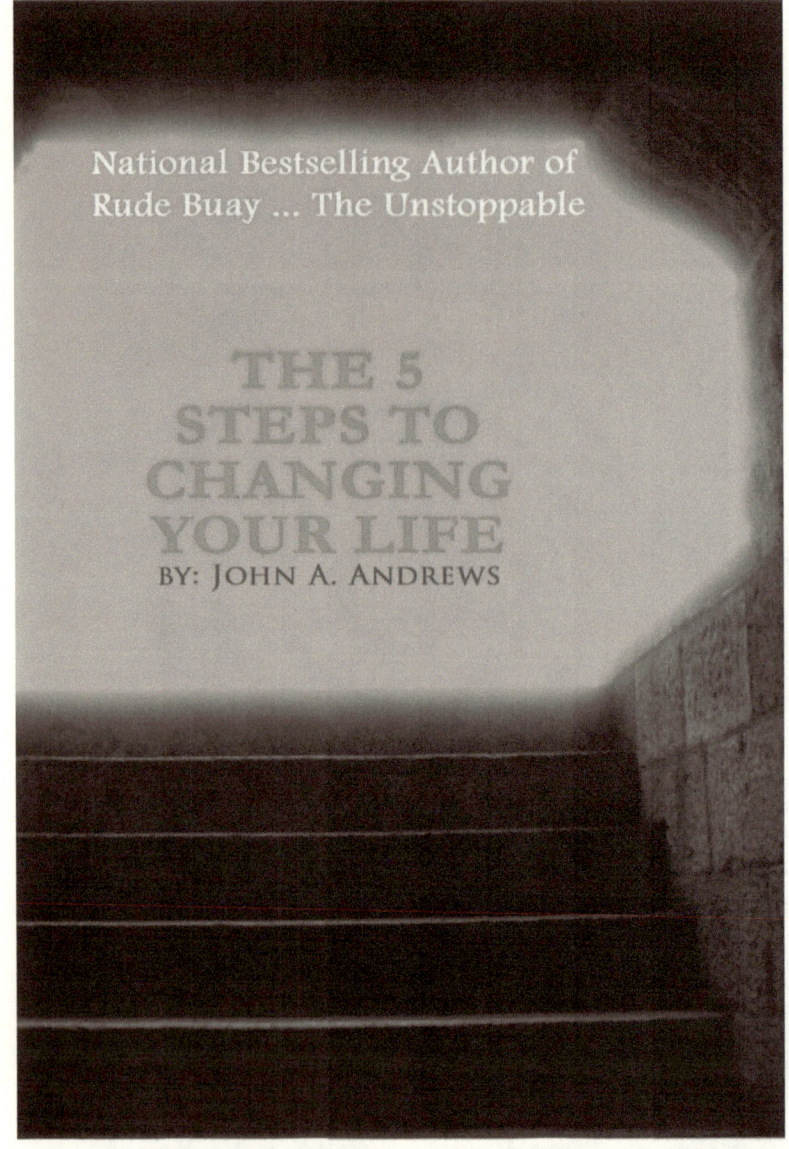

National Bestselling Author of
Rude Buay ... The Unstoppable

THE 5
STEPS TO
CHANGING
YOUR LIFE
BY: JOHN A. ANDREWS

DARE TO MAKE A DIFFERENCE
SUCCESS 101 FOR TEENS

THE 5 Ps FOR TEENS

SPREAD SOME LOVE – RELATIONSHIPS 101

TOTAL COMMITMENT

<u>WHOSE WOMAN WAS SHE?</u>

WHEN THE DUST SETTLES –
I AM STILL STANDING

CHICO RUDO ... EL IMPARABLE

<u>RUDE BUAY ... THE UNSTOPPABLE</u>
<u>CHINESE EDITION</u>

VISIT: **WWW.JOHNAANDREWS.COM**

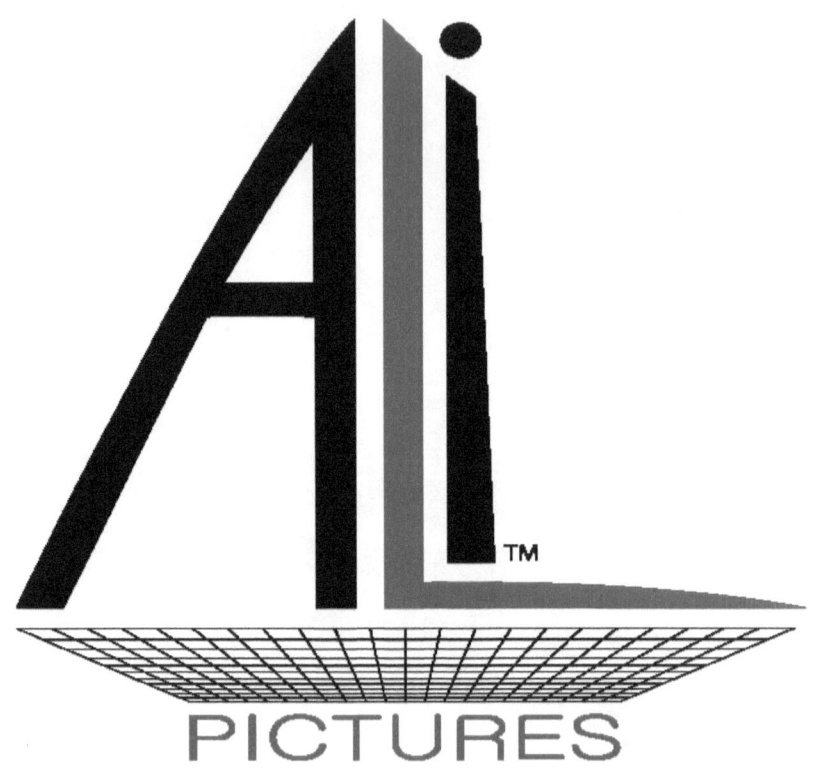

Optioned by A L I Pictures, LLC.

LIKE Us on FaceBook

https://www.facebook.com/Whoshotthesherifffilm

www.ingramcontent.com/pod-product-compliance
Lightning Source LLC
Chambersburg PA
CBHW030543030726
47495CB00004B/1117